Penguin Books
The Buffalo Soldiers

John Prebble was born in Middlesex in 1915 but spent his boyhood in Saskatchewan, Canada. A journalist since 1934, he is also a novelist, film-writer, and the author of several highly praised dramatized documentaries for B.B.C. television and radio. During the war he served six years in the ranks with the Royal Artillery, from which experience he wrote his successful war novel, *The Edge of Darkness*. His other books include *Where the Sea Breaks*, *The Buffalo Soldiers*, which won an award in the United States for the best historical novel of the American West, and *Culloden*, a subject he became interested in when he was a boy in a predominantly Scottish township in Canada. *Culloden* was published in 1963 and *Glencoe* in the Spring of 1966. All these books are available in Penguins. His latest book is *The Lion in the North* (Penguin, 1971).

John Prebble

The Buffalo Soldiers

Penguin Books

Penguin Books Ltd,
Harmondsworth, Middlesex, England
Penguin Books Australia Ltd,
Ringwood, Victoria, Australia
Penguin Books Canada Ltd,
41 Steelcase Road West, Markham, Ontario, Canada
Penguin Books (N.Z.) Ltd,
182–190 Wairau Road, Auckland 10, New Zealand

First published by Martin Secker & Warburg 1959
Published in Penguin Books 1975

Made and printed in Great Britain by
Richard Clay (The Chaucer Press) Ltd,
Bungay, Suffolk
Set in Linotype Pilgrim

'But there are things which you have said to me which I do not like. They were not sweet like sugar but bitter like gourds. You said that you wanted to put us upon a reservation, to build us houses and make us medicine lodges. I do not want them. I was born where the wind blew free and there was nothing to break the light of the sun. I was born where there were no enclosures and everything drew a free breath. I want to die there and not within walls. So why do you ask us to leave the rivers, and the sun, and the wind, and live in houses? Do not ask us to give up the buffalo for the sheep. The young men have heard talk of this, and it has made them sad and angry. The whites have the country which we loved, and we only wish to wander on the prairie until we die. Any good thing you say to me shall not be forgotten . . .'

—*Ten Bears, Comanche spokesman*, 1867.

The sky was black. Men and horses turned their faces away from the rain, pushing their left shoulders into it and moving forward like crabs. Water ran between the collar of the lieutenant's blouse and his neck, chafing the flesh. It gathered in the brim of his hat and spouted from the peak when he bent his head. The yellow teeth of his horse snarled at the bit, and the reek of its breath hardened his weary resentment of any demand on his attention.

Agent Tatum, riding at the lieutenant's right hand, persistently made such a demand. His feet slipped from the stirrup-treads, leaving his legs kicking and he swayed on the unfamiliar saddle. A man so inept, thought the lieutenant, should give all his time to the control of his horse, but Tatum talked anxiously, clutching at his hat with one hand and bending forward to look into the lieutenant's face. His words were jerked from his soft lips by the jolting of his body. 'Thee must not misunderstand,' he said, for the third time since leaving the post. 'The precepts of the Society oppose the use of soldiers. Nor can I wholly approve of this hunt.'

The lieutenant nodded shortly, and water once more ran from his hat. He raised himself a little in the saddle and stared ahead, more to discourage the agent than to see anything, for there was nothing beyond and about them but the grey fall of the rain.

'I have told them that there is land for them to plough.'

'Don't pull on the leathers, Mr Tatum, give the horse its head.'

'I thank thee. The Caddoes and Wichitas have raised melons and beans.'

'So I've heard.'

7

'But the soldiers steal the vegetables.'

Feeling none, the lieutenant offered no sympathy.

'I shall give an annual prize of five hundred dollars to the ten Indians who raise the best harvest, and there is the steam-engine from Chicago for the saw-mill.' Tatum seemed about to fall from the horse altogether, but grasped its mane and saved himself. The lieutenant swallowed the oath that had risen in his throat.

'Yes sir, I've heard of that too.'

The earth took them down suddenly, throwing Tatum back against the cantle. His hat fell off, and they halted until a trooper had recovered it. Mud was yellow on the crown, but Tatum seemed unaware of it. There was mud on his face, too.

'What is thy name, lieutenant? I was not told.'

'It's Byrne.'

'Thee is an Irishman,' said Tatum, less as a question than an acknowledgement. 'And a Catholic too, I imagine.'

Now may you be damned for a Quaker farmer! But as he looked at the agent the lieutenant immediately regretted the thought. Tatum's round face shone with rain, and his eyes were half-closed, his teeth clenched against the force of it. 'If you are going to talk to me, Mr Tatum, won't you ride on my left? That way you'll not look into the weather.'

'I thank thee, but it's of no consequence. Would not the rain then be in thy face?'

'It was just a suggestion,' said Byrne stiffly. Then, because the man's obvious discomfort irked him, he said, 'They shouldn't have given you a trooper's horse and saddle. You're not used to them.'

'It's of no consequence, though I asked for a mule. The soldier didn't understand.'

'I guess not,' said Byrne with the picture in his mind.

'He was an African. Does it delight thee to command these Africans, lieutenant?'

'Africans? Oh, you mean the troopers.' Byrne looked over his shoulder to the patrol, and saw it hunched miserably beneath wet ponchos, the rise and fall of rain-black hats. He wiped the palm of his hand from brow to chin in one abrupt movement.

8

'I can't say they delight me at the moment. The Tenth Nubian Horse,' he said.

Tatum shook his head. 'Thy levity is unkind . . .'

Why should the man misunderstand, or was he in fact understanding? 'No levity was intended, Mr Tatum. An ex-slave might do worse than enlist.'

'There is the earth for them to plough.'

'You're pulling at the leathers again, sir. The horse knows the pace, it won't run away with you.'

'I thank thee. It would be better for them not to be soldiers at all.'

'It's an opinion, sir,' agreed Byrne. He stood in the stirrups and punched the air with his fist to increase the gait of the rear files, and saw one of the pack-mules slide splay-legged at the sudden pull of its lead-rope.

'I mean', said Tatum, shouting now, his face knotted against the rain, and a white hand waving, 'that they should not be forced into the Army.'

'It was their choice. Shouldn't we be meeting your Indians soon?'

Tatum pointed ahead. 'It's difficult to see. But there, they should be waiting there now.'

'We'll have to wait for them, damn their pride. How many?'

'A dozen perhaps,' said Tatum uncertainly. 'The agency chiefs said there would be young men, and women to help. It's not my plan that they should hunt buffalo again, Mr Byrne, but the Army has sent them no food.'

The complaint was querulous and unreasonable, springing from a civilian's latent dislike of the military, and Byrne thought that Tatum, an honest agent, should at least know better. He answered roughly. 'Why should the Army correct the mistakes of the Indian Office? Anyway, your friends would rather hunt and steal and murder than plant your crops.'

'In God's time they shall be taught.'

'Yes sir.' The rain was slackening. Half a mile away trees emerged from the fog of it, a file of cottonwoods escorting the creek, clouded with leaves, their white roots washed free from the sandy bottom. 'There?'

9

'I believe so, but can thee see anyone?'

Byrne raised his hand, and heard the patrol halt behind them, a ring of metal, a squeal of stretching stirrup-straps, the slap of mules' hooves. A deep voice, reverberating in cavernous lungs, said *Glory be!* And the rain stopped. Sunlight broke on one end of the valley, moving swiftly forward in flood, over the trees and the harsh hills until it enveloped the patrol. The sky was blue again, and the wide land coloured with muted browns and yellows. Men lifted their faces, and in the sudden heat they and their horses smoked with steam. Agent Tatum took off his tall hat and shook it. His bald head was like a ripe apple.

Byrne called without turning. 'Sergeant!'

A man in the first file pushed forward his horse to the lieutenant's side, throwing back his poncho to show the bars on his sleeve. He was a mulatto, young and thin-nosed, with the kind of face, Byrne thought, that reminded one of a well-honed knife. His watchful eyes were as disconcerting as the musical challenge of his voice. 'Peter Salem. First Sergeant, Company M. Tenth Cavalry. Sir.'

'All right. Dismount and picket for grazing. They can make coffee, I suppose. Can you find me a striker?' He dismounted himself, and was almost knocked to the ground as Tatum fell against him, striking him heavily between the shoulders. 'Dismount from the other side of the horse, sir. The animal expects it. Are you all right?'

'I thank thee. But I did not intend to alight that way.' Tatum began to wipe his face with a blue handkerchief, gouging his eyes with it and rubbing his neck vigorously, and all the while looking at Byrne curiously. 'Thee is a stranger to these men?'

'I know none of them. I'm new to the regiment.' He paused, and added, without knowing why he thought the agent needed to know, 'I'm new to officer's rank also, Mr Tatum.'

'There should be no vanity in rank, Mr Byrne.'

'I have none, sir,' said Byrne, regretting the confidence. He faced the sergeant who had returned with a short, fat trooper whose body seemed boneless in its uniform, as if the blue flannel had been inflated. The boy stood with his drawers showing above the waistband of his trousers, his fingers extended and pressed against his thighs. He is almost a caricature, thought Byrne, the darky in the illustration on a sentimental song-sheet. The lift of his cheeks by his white-toothed smile almost closed his eyes. 'What's your name?'

'Crispin Cometoliberty, sir.'

'You name yourself, bub?'

'Yes *sir*, in the year of Jubilo!'

'You'll answer to Crispin, it's shorter.'

Salem's voice was softly critical. 'His *master* called him Crispin, sir. A liveryman in Savannah. He beat Crispin.'

'Beat me two, three times a week,' agreed the boy.

'All right. Thank you. Do you know what a striker is?'

'Means the lieutenant's servant, sir.'

'Then get on with it. I want coffee for Mr Tatum and myself, and I want it as black as your . . .' He saw the quick clouding of Salem's eyes. 'You want something, sergeant?'

'Black as my damned hide, yes sir,' said Crispin. 'Yes *sir*!'

'No,' said Byrne, 'just black. What's your complaint, Sergeant Salem?'

'There's no complaint, lieutenant,' said Salem in a gentle voice, and he saluted and turned away.

Byrne took off his hat and stared down the valley. There was an iridescent sheen where the distant grass met the sky, and the heat was heavy and implacable. He wiped his sleeve across his forehead, and at the end of the movement he saw that Tatum, too, was staring at him. 'Yes?' he said.

'Thee has gloried in the freed slave, Mr Byrne?'

'Something like that, I suppose.'

The Indian agent nodded. He rubbed the palms of his hands together, as if evaluating the lieutenant's answer, and he held his head to one side, smiling faintly.

'Loosen the girth of your saddle, please,' said Byrne coldly, and he turned his attention to the patrol. Two troopers were digging a coffee trench, the others were scraping great balls of mud from the hooves of their horses, and when he grumbled at them unreasonably they smiled, opened their eyes wide, jerked their heads and took the sting out of his criticism with their own good humour. Laughter rippled out of their whispers when he turned his back on them, and although he knew that it was not directed at him he felt a tightness in his chest and an aggressive tilt to his chin.

Salem was waiting for him. Dismounted, the mulatto was nearly seven inches taller than Byrne, his body supple and narrow-hipped, one knee bent and a thumb hooked in his belt. The shadow of his hat was blue on his olive face, and within it his eyes were black and meditative. His upper lip was beaded with sweat, which he wiped away before he saluted. The salute was a casual, almost insulting recognition of military propriety. Byrne pointed to the half-chevron on the man's cuff. 'Your second enlistment?'

'Yes sir. I served with the 54th Massachusetts Infantry. I was at the assault on Fort Wagner with Colonel Shaw.' He said this sardonically rather than with pride, as if he suspected that the information would confound Byrne and wished to see what effect it would have. It was the tone of his voice that provoked the officer's harsh reply. 'What of it?'

Salem straightened his back, and his eyes looked across the top of Byrne's head. 'The lieutenant has heard of the action?'

'I've heard of it. And I accept the inference that you must be something of a soldier.'

'That wasn't my meaning, sir. Have I your permission to speak?'

'You're a damned talkative sergeant as it is, Salem.'

'Yes sir. I've heard the lieutenant knows something about sergeants.'

Byrne laughed, reluctantly admiring the man's impudence. 'All right. It's no secret I was one myself, if that's what you mean. Now what's your comment?'

'That Colonel Shaw didn't find it hard to command men of colour.'

'I've heard he considered it something of an honour.'

'Yes sir. That's what I meant.'

Byrne looked at the mulatto silently. He listened to the music of the water in the valley, the sneeze of a horse, and a voice softly singing. He was not angry. He was curious. 'Sergeant, I don't give a damn about your colour. Will you oblige me by not giving a damn about mine?'

'I don't give a damn about your colour, Lieutenant.'

'Thank you. And you might as well know that at the moment I see no honour in commanding this patrol.'

'All but three are recruits, sir.'

'I know that. In five minutes you tighten girths and take them up there on the rim and start making soldiers out of them, understood? Right and left front into line at the walk. Understood?'

'Yes sir.'

Byrne called him back, in a gentler voice. 'Salem, as I recall it the 54th was a regiment of freed men. Were you never a slave?'

'I was a slave, sir.' The mulatto now looked into Byrne's eyes, but without expression. 'I had an enlightened owner, I was told. I was taught to read and write, and I have some knowledge of mathematics, physics, French and Spanish. I can also read music.'

'I'll be damned!'

'Yes sir.'

Grinning stupidly, Bryne walked across to Tatum. The agent was sitting on his heels, crouched like a frog, his knees tight against his trousers and wide, his vest unbuttoned and his head shining above his tufted hair. It was his tall hat, resting upright on the grass before him, that really made him look incongruous. He held up a tin cup. 'Whatever the colour of thy servant's skin, Mr Byrne, he will make good coffee for thee.'

The soft rebuke escaped Byrne. He sat down, looking across the valley, and then he laughed, hitting his thigh with his hand. 'I've got a sergeant who's better educated than most lieutenants, including myself.'

Tatum rubbed the crown of his head vigorously. 'How old is thee, Mr Byrne?'

'I'm thirty-eight. Does that prove something for you?'

'Perhaps. I have been watching thee, and wondering, and knowledge of a man's age is the beginning of an understanding of him. Thy temper is hot, but is there any hate in thee?'

13

The directness of the question uncovered memories, and it seemed to Byrne that he could see his father's face again, and hear the passion of his voice. 'No sir,' he said honestly, 'there's no hate in me. That should please you.'

'I do not know, Mr Byrne, for it may mean that there is no love in thee also.'

Byrne pushed a spur into the earth and laughed. 'Mr Tatum, for a man as clever as you contrive to be, how is it that you're so wrong about the Comanche?'

The agent was not offended. 'Am I wrong? We shall try, and we shall make many mistakes, and we shall do God's work in the end.'

'God's work to make the Comanche and Kiowa plough and live in houses like the Caddoes?'

'God's work, and His will for all men. And we have many Comanche on the reservation.'

Byrne shook his head, and he poured the dregs of his coffee from the cup, as if by way of an illustration. 'A handful of Kwahadis who want free meals and agency blankets for a while. You could lose them tomorrow, for they are none too happy about the sacrifice of their manhood.'

'There is no manhood in fighting, Mr Byrne.'

'It's an opinion, sir.'

The patrol rode by.

Now God damn them! Byrne stood up with his fists on his hips and his short legs astride. The troopers bobbed and jostled, lifting their buttocks and leaning forward. Answering the right moulinet of Salem's arm they broke from column, but the effort to swing into line resulted in an ugly knot of confusion. Byrne hit his hip with a fist, and he heard the thin blasphemy of Salem's voice above the thudding of hooves. Three times the movement was attempted, and with the fourth Byrne let his breath pass slowly between his teeth. *Better!*

Although the sight of a Negro on a horse still seemed to him to be a vague contradiction, like seeing a woman in man's clothes, he was surprised to discover that he was pleased by the professional challenge of this command. He thrust his thumbs into his waistband and slapped the fingers against his stomach, lifting his head and looking about him. There was now a warm wind moving, heavy with the scent of scarlet flowers on the grass flats, and humming with the sound of cicadas. The eastern wall of the valley was a thousand yards away, and on its crimped and yellow folds lay triangles of dark shadow. Between this and the creek the tall grass shuddered, ripples running northward until they were lost in the haze below the suspended islands of the Wichita Mountains.

A white-eyed trooper came down the rise with arms stiff, bouncing in the saddle as if all that kept him there was the lock of his boots in the stirrups. 'Indians,' he said, jerking a finger down the valley.

'All right, bub. How many?'

The tongue-thickened slur of the man's voice made it hard to understand. 'Dozen, maybe. Mile, two mile off, lieutenant, sir.'

Tatum hurried forward, buttoning his vest with one hand and forcing down his hat with the other. 'Is there one with a red blanket? That will be Quasia, that will be a young man called Eagle-Tail-Feather, Mr Byrne. The agency chiefs said he would be the leader.'

Byrne mounted and twirled his hat to recall the patrol, and when it had returned he looked at it, deliberately composing his face into an expression of disgust. The troopers grinned back at him through their sweat, or pulled in their bellies and frowned. He said, 'Which one of you is Christian Veal?' A stocky rider, with a chest so arched that it seemed a deformity, a brown face with high cheek-bones, flapped a hand to his hat-brim and said '*Yo!*' He wore a red and white bandanna instead of cavalry mustard, and his straight hair hung over his ears. 'You're part Wichita, I was told, and you're to do my talking for me when our friends come up here. You'll say what I say and not what suits your fancy. Understood?'

'Lieutenant,' said Tatum, slipping on the grass as he jerked his body forward anxiously, 'thee will have no need of Christian Veal.'

Byrne looked down at the agent, with his hand on the cantle of the saddle, and his body lifted. 'Mr Tatum,' he said heavily. 'I do not want your advice on the conduct of this patrol.'

'As it pleases thee, sir,' said Tatum equably.

'That's how it pleases me,' said Byrne. He crossed his hands at the groin and stared at the troopers. He saw their dark faces and melancholy eyes, the newness of navy flannel, the hardness of unworn boots, the grey felt hats ungreased by wear. He looked at them and tried to forget the memory of white men in the same uniform. The black soldiers looked at him, and what they saw was a small-statured, long-armed man with heavy hands, a thick neck on which the flesh had been wrinkled and coarse-grained by weather, a face that appeared both comical and noble because of its broken nose and the deep cleft in its chin.

'Salem, names and service.'

His eyes on the horizon, the sergeant called each name, and the answering cries of '*Yo-o-o!*' spanned an octave.

'Jonathan Attucks. Corporal. Second Enlistment . . .

'Absalom Riddle. Trumpeter. Second Enlistment . . .

'Christian Veal. Private. Five months . . .

'George Honesty. Private. Three months . . .

'Nathan Donethegetaway. Private. Three months . . .'

'One moment,' said Byrne. 'How old are you?'

The man pushed back his hat and smiled sadly out of his charcoal-grey face. His hair was frosted on his skull and his watering eyes heavily pouched. He held a hand before his face, as if he expected to find an answer between the long, flattened fingers. Attucks leant over and said hoarsely, 'How old are you, Uncle?'

'Done thought 'bout it plenty times.' He looked at Byrne slily. 'Thirty, maybe?'

'He run away to Canady,' said 'Attucks, grinning, 'Lieutenant, sir. Got nigh to freedom afore he was catched.'

'All right.' Byrne nodded to Salem.

'Salvation Calhoun. Private. Three months . . .

'Miles James. Private. Two months . . .

'Crispin Cometoliberty. Private. Two months . . .

'Virgil Conception. Private. Two months . . .'

Byrne sighed and stared down the creek. The sunlight trembled nervously on the leaves of the cottonwoods, but there was no sign of the Indians. He faced the patrol again. 'The Comanche', he said, 'are rightly considered the finest horsemen on the plains.' And he wondered if the information made any appeal to their pride. 'Attucks!'

The corporal came slowly forward with arrogant confidence, one hand above the pommel and holding the reins, his knees controlling the horse without effort. He was erect, broad at the shoulders and very black. The front brim of his hat had been turned up, his brow was furrowed and he had a great jut of a jaw. He passed his tongue pinkly along his lips and then half-closed his eyes. Byrne was faintly impressed.

'Now listen to me. You are horse-soldiers, and according to the manual that is how a horse-soldier sits. Body balanced in the middle of your mount's back, head erect and square to the front, chin in, chest out, elbows to the rear of the points of the shoulders. Understood?'

Their concentration, he thought, was childishly willing, heads tilted, eyes narrowed. Nathan Donethegetaway nodded, pushed back his hat and scratched his head.

'Understood?' said Byrne. 'The leathers come into the left hand on the side of the little finger, and leave between the thumb and forefinger. Hold your hand up, Attucks. The little finger is between the reins, right rein above it, the other fingers closed, thumb pressing the reins firmly on the second joint of the forefinger. *Understood?* The left forearm is horizontal and close to the body, wrist turned inward so that the back of the hand is almost perpendicular to the front.'

Now he was looking down to the creek again. 'That's what the manual says, and that's what I want to see always. The right hand hangs naturally behind the thigh, and your feet are in the stirrups so that the ball rests on the tread and the heel is lowered. Understood?'

There was a movement in the trees. A flash of vivid colour. The high yelping of a dog.

'Left front. Into line, ho-o!' Their enthusiasm made a mockery of the movement. *God damn you all!*

The Indians were in no hurry. Some rode on the bank, backs bent to pass beneath the trees, and others rode in the creek

17

itself, their ponies high-stepping with heads lifted. The shadows and the sunlight broke across them so that they appeared and disappeared until at last they turned on to the grass, and a yellow dog yapped and spun about them. Byrne counted. Ten, and two women walking beside travois-dragging mules. It was some seconds before he realized that the ululating sound he could hear came from a singing throat. A hundred yards from the patrol the party halted, motionless and erect, the wind teasing feathers and buckskin fringes, and the dog still snapping and snarling until one of the women struck it with a stick.

When the song stopped, bouncing on a dying echo, the foremost Indian draped his scarlet blanket across the withers of his horse and held up both hands, palms towards the troopers. Thus he remained until Byrne repeated the greeting and then, one by one, the Indians slipped to the ground, squatting in the shade of their ponies.

'*Veal!*' Byrne dismounted and walked down the grass, pushing his body forward with the determined thrust of his shoulders, conscious of a frown tightening between his eyes, and hearing the frantic hop and skip as Tatum hurried to keep pace with him. When he reached the Indians he sat himself on the ground before them, his legs tucked awkwardly beneath him. Tatum sat on his right, breathing hard and wiping his face vigorously again. No word was spoken, the water ran and the cicadas throbbed, and, mixed with the sweet perfume of the flowers, Byrne now smelt the strong odour of the Indians, the acrid sting of animal fat and warm flesh.

Quasia was a slight young man with glass beads in his long hair, his lips thin, his nose sharp and his face round and smooth like a cheese. He was the warm, generous colour of polished copper, his deep chest naked, the muscles hard on his arms and shoulders. The intelligence of his eyes was cold and distant enough to be faintly hostile. A single black and white feather slanted across the back of his head, held there by an animal's claw. His right hand cradled a repeating rifle, and the left played with the rawhide bridle that passed in two half-hitches about the lower jaw of his horse. The animal stirred Byrne's admiration, a red-eyed, yellow beast with black mane, tail and feet. Its nostrils had been slit to make it longer-winded, and blue circles were painted on its flanks.

The other Indians were as young, or younger than Quasia, their faces less impassive, and they stared curiously at the black troopers beyond Byrne's shoulder. One, whose face was hideously pock-marked, and who was fat enough to look like a naked woman, grinned idiotically and made an obscene movement with his thumbs.

Quasia spoke, rich and sonorous sounds that scarcely moved his lips but which came powerfully from his throat. A woman, young and short-haired, shapeless in an army-blue blanket stamped USID, placed something in his hand. He held the hand out to Byrne, and on the light-skinned palm were two corn-shuck cigarettes rolled in twenty-five cent shin-plasters. They smoked, and although Byrne felt as though his lungs had suddenly been ignited he endeavoured to keep his face still. The blue smoke dribbled from Quasia's nostrils, and he sucked it back into his mouth. He seemed proud of his skill and did this several times, holding the cigarette between thumb and fore-finger, the way Byrne had seen Mexicans smoke.

'Veal. Tell him my name. Tell him I have heard of him from Agent Tatum, and what I've heard I like.'

Quasia looked at the Indian agent as he might have looked at a stone.

'Tell him my orders are to escort his party on a hunt for meat, but it may not cross the Red into Texas, and that we must return in five days, whether buffalo is found or not.'

'No,' said Quasia calmly.

Tatum sighed, like a parent faced with a wilful child at last aware of its foolishness. 'That is what I wished to tell thee, Mr Byrne. Quasia speaks English.'

'Ourfatherwhichartinheaven,' said Quasia.

Tatum shook his head unhappily. 'He was sent to the Colville Indian School in Pennsylvania after the Fitzpatrick treaty was signed. It wasn't much of a success.'

Quasia held a fist in the air passionately. 'Beat! Every day boys beat with narrow sticks. I leave.' For some seconds he sat with his back straight, his chest rising and falling, and then he said to Byrne, 'You say Ourfatherwhichartinheaven?'

'I can say it.'

Quasia nodded, and stared morosely at the earth between them. He pointed to Veal and spoke quickly in his own tongue.

'Lieutenant, he says if them buffalo are over the Red he'll go after them. Says hunt may take two weeks.'

'Tell him our forage won't run to it.'

'He says our horses must be as weak as we are. Comanche ponies don't carry no food.'

'Tell him the Caddoes have seen the Texas Herd of buffalo north of the Red, plenty of them.'

'He says white hunters have slaughtered it.'

'Tell him the Army has ordered all white hunters to stay north of the Arkansas.'

Quasia did not wait to be told, he sneered, and cut his hand sharply across the front of his body.

Byrne leant forward, and prodded the air with his finger. 'Quasia, you heard what I said. There'll be no raiding into Texas. If you do we'll have to go after you and fight.'

The Indian said nothing. He looked at the cigarette in his hand, closed his fingers about it and let the pieces fall to the grass. Tatum began to wave his hands, as if he were brushing flies from his face. 'Young man, listen to me. I am thy friend, listen to me. When this hunt is over thee will learn to plough the earth and grow food . . .'

Quasia curled his lip and spoke over his shoulder to the others, and an eddy of anger passed among them. 'Mr Tatum, sir,' said Veal, 'he says The People don't stick knives into their mother.'

One of the Comanches began to shout, working himself into a temper, and chopping the air with a straight palm. It was the fat, pock-marked boy, and his anger took the lazy good-humour from his face. 'Now,' said Byrne, raising his voice, 'we'll ride now. You can cut your own trail, Quasia. The Cad-does reported the herd there, two days ago.' He pointed to the west. He put out his hand. 'Let it be a good hunt.' Quasia looked at the hand for some time before he took it. His grip was firm, but without warmth.

'No,' he said, and spoke again in his own language.

'Lieutenant, sir, he says tomorrow. Tomorrow on account of having to make medicine in the morning. Lieutenant, sir, I don't understand too good.'

'*Damn him!*'

Quasia smiled and placed a hand on Byrne's wrist.

'Begging the lieutenant's pardon, sir,' said Veal, a faint note of amusement in his voice, 'but it's what he says. Says your anger is like a lance in a weak man's hand.'

'Then damn his poetic images!' Byrne's face was flushed. The Comanche calmly caressed his pony's foreleg, placing his cheek against its lowered muzzle. Byrne got up suddenly and stamped back towards the troopers. Half-way he stopped. Tatum and Veal were hurrying after him, the agent waving his hat in disapproval. The Indians had not moved. 'All right, then,' shouted Byrne. 'You can tell him it's tomorrow!'

Agent Tatum returned to the post two hours later. He was unwilling to go. His face open, his eyes blinking, and his body sweating uncomfortably in its black broadcloth, he declared that he should stay until the morning, that he should talk to Quasia, for the young man was stiff-necked and proud, and in need of Christian advice. Byrne, wearied by the Quaker and yet curiously impressed by the man's innocent zeal, shook his head. He would be obliged if Tatum left as soon as possible, and took with him a report for Alvord. The report was merely an excuse, but having been suggested it had to be written.

He sat on his saddle with his back to the patrol and tore a sheet of paper from his notebook, wetting the stub of pencil with his tongue. The first words he wrote were, inevitably, a blurred smear before his eyes, and he wondered why he was fool enough not to admit that this would happen always. From a leather case in the pocket of his blouse he took a pair of gold-rimmed spectacles, fumbling clumsily as he looped them over his ears. He could see the writing now, but who had ever seen a cavalryman in spectacles, below the rank of general, that is?

At least it was better to have long sight than short, but the spectacles kept slipping down the broken bridge of his nose until he bent the arms to hold them.

To Captain Henry Alvord,
Cdg Company M,
Regt H.Q. Tenth (Coloured) Cavalry,
Fort Sill, Ind. Terr.

Sir: I have made contact with the Comanche buffalo party eight miles south of the post on Cache Creek. There are ten men and two women led by Eagle-Tail-Feather. He speaks some English. They refuse to leave here before morning. In view of the fact that all but three of my command are recruits, and as advised by you this morning, I shall employ the time profitably with training. The agent, Mr Tatum, will be able to give you any information not relevant to this report.

G. A. Byrne, Lt.

When he had shaken Tatum's hand, and nodded away advice on treatment of the Indians, he watched the Quaker ride off suddenly displeased by the realization that he was now the only white man there, and that to the loneliness of command was added this exclusion by colour. He resented it, not so much from moral principles as from a stubborn annoyance with something hitherto inexperienced. There was a question in his mind. When you swear at a Negro are you swearing at him or the colour of his skin? And if you are swearing at him, will he still think it is his black skin you hate? Do you always have to be polite to them, damn them?

The smoke of the Comanche fires was filling the valley. Beyond the trees were the brown, white, black and yellow splashes of the close-hobbled ponies, tails sweeping at the flies. The Indians were sitting below the largest tree, playing some sort of hand-game. They sang gambling-songs, and one of the women beat time with a stick on a parfleche. They laughed, and made as much noise as men in a saloon, and Byrne wondered who the fool was who had created this fiction of the impassive, taciturn savage.

He turned to the troopers. Most of them lay on their backs

together, hats over their eyes, their long legs bent so that they looked like stands of arms. Their indolence pricked Byrne's regimental pride, and he told Salem to mount them and take them up on the rim again. He watched, with his feet astride, his thick hands tightly clasped behind his rigid back, and he felt the sweat trickling down the furrow of his neck to his shoulder-blades. When the sergeant began to call the singing cavalry orders there was a momentary silence among the Comanches. They turned their heads to look for a moment or two, and then they returned to their game.

For half an hour Byrne watched the patrol before he recalled it. He expected sullen faces and frowns, the natural and inevitable reaction of white troopers, but the Negroes came down with bright smiles, like children asking for praise. He cried out in disgust.

'Sergeant, what in hell's name are those men taking their mounts to water for? Cool them down first!' He thrust his hands into his waistband and chewed his lips, and then, 'They did well enough, Salem. You can tell them that if you wish.'

'Would the lieutenant care to tell them?'

'He would not. Picket on the line and graze early when dew's on the grass. I want leather and arms cleaned.'

He went to where Crispin had laid out his saddle and blanket, and he took a cheroot from the bag and chewed the end meditatively for five minutes before lighting it. The sun was dropping, and in the cooling air the Comanches had abandoned their hand-game and were playing kick-the-ball. He walked down to watch them.

The ball was a bundle of skins tightly bound with rawhide. When thrown to a man who stood with his right foot lifted he caught it on the instep, struck it into the air, and hopped forward to hit it again before it fell to the ground. The pock-marked boy, despite his fat, was able to keep the ball in the air for fifty or sixty yards while the others whooped. When the Indians at last noticed that Byrne was watching them they were silent. He did not move, but stared back at them, and just as he was beginning to feel that this boy's game of stare-down was being carried beyond his dignity, Quasia picked up the ball and threw it into the air. It landed heavily by Byrne's right instep. The fat Comanche called out a derisive challenge.

Byrne stared at the ball with embarrassment, moving the cheroot from one side of his mouth to the other, and then he turned about and walked stiffly up the hill. He knew that perhaps he should have accepted the challenge, but, *damn it*, a grown man did not play boys' games. But it was a mistake, made unconsciously, like that business of Crispin and the coffee. He was always making mistakes like that, and he did not know what he could do about it. Nor, perhaps, did it really matter.

He took a towel and razor and went down to the creek. He cut himself twice and he threw water on his cheek to congeal the blood, staring at his reflection sourly. He heard Salem's call for sentries, and he looked back and saw a trooper, carbine slanted, climbing the rise, and another beginning his slow pace along the horse-lines. Attucks was singing. Dusk came down the valley quickly, a blue dusk in which the pink fires glowed and the scent of wood-smoke was stronger. Over on the grass flats fire-flies sparked at waist height, and the neigh of a cavalry-mount was answered by a nicker from the Indian ponies. And then, suddenly, it was very dark.

Still he did not move, growing cold, the wet end of the dead cheroot foul on his tongue. He threw it away at last and walked up to the bivouac, beyond it to the sentry on the rise. When the man challenged, Byrne said, 'What's your name?'

'Conception, sir.' Byrne struck a match to light another cigar, and held the flame a moment longer to see the soldier's face. The man's brows were set high on his forehead, slanting upward to the centre, and giving him a permanent expression of alarm and dismay. He was shivering slightly.

'What's the matter, are you cold? I'll send a blanket up to you.' He remembered. 'Virgil Conception, isn't it? How old are you, boy?'

'Ain't nobody never told me, sir.'

Nineteen, thought Byrne, thirteen or fourteen when Mr Lincoln freed the slaves in the year of Jubilo, and then he realized that the boy was not shivering with cold, but with fear. He did not know what to say. The match was out and they were in darkness again. At last he said roughly, 'Do your duty, boy.'

There was a shot from the bivouac. And then shouts, feet racing at great speed and halting abruptly. Someone piled brush on a fire and the valley came alive in yellow light. Byrne saw two figures, half-way between the bivouac and the Comanche camp, rolling and scuffling on the ground. He ran towards them, his fingers tugging unsuccessfully with the button of his pistol holster and cursing it. He reached the fighting men before he could loosen the weapon, and he bent down with hands grasping, his fingers clutching first at the naked shoulder of an Indian and then at the flannel blouse of a trooper. This he grasped, seeing below him dimly an arm with a knife, an arm with a pistol. He pulled, and then he heard Quasia's voice, calling sharply. The Indian below wriggled free and stood up, his braided hair loosened, teeth showing, and the knife still hanging from his hand.

The trooper began to stammer, 'Private Honesty, sir . . .'

'Damn it, what happened here?'

'He was asnooping round the horses, lieutenant . . .'

'You the sentry there? Where's your carbine? What the hell were you trying to do? The man was curious about our horse-flesh that's all. Were you trying to kill him? Damn you, Honesty, were you looking for medals?'

'Begging the lieutenant's pardon . . .'

'Shut your damned mouth!'

Now all the fires were flaming, and the Comanches had come up, and some had weapons in their hands. Salem called, and Byrne heard the clicking of carbine locks. 'Salem,' he said, very weary, 'ground those carbines.'

He called for Veal. 'Tell them I won't have any of them about our lines after dark. Say they risk getting shot.'

'Sir, don't he understand you?'

'Tell them, I want them all to know.'

When Veal had finished, punching home the uncertain words with sign-language, none of the Indians moved. Quasia looked carefully at the angry little officer, and then he turned to the Comanche who had been fighting, speaking to him quickly and passionately. The man's answer was surly, and Quasia took a brass axe from his waist and knocked him to the ground with its haft. He looked from the unconscious figure to the soldiers, staring particularly at Honesty.

'Veal. Tell him we do not strike our soldiers.'

Quasia shrugged his shoulders.

'Honesty,' said Byrne, 'you're supposed to be a horse-soldier, but tomorrow you can find out what it's like to be in the infantry. You'll walk beside your horse all the way till noon. That's a punishment and it'll be entered on report. You've a right to know you can enter a complaint under Article Thirty if you wish.' He turned his back on the surprised Negro. 'Veal, tell them how I'm punishing this fool. Make them understand what it means to a trooper.'

Quasia listened. Then he tightened the red blanket about his hips, and left without speaking.

Dawn, with the mist deep in the valley. Byrne awoke to the barking of the Indian dog, and he lay for some seconds with his mind suspended between sleep and consciousness. Then he pushed himself on to one elbow, rubbing the palm of his hand over his face brutally, and he saw that the mist was so close to the ground that the tops of the trees appeared to be floating on it. The air was cold, and he shivered. He was awake quickly, and angry with the ache of bone and muscle, angry at lost youth, angry at anger itself. The emotion passed through him and left his mind clear. As the sun rose the grey mist became white, and then warm gold, disappearing rapidly.

He saw the line of sleeping troopers and, as always, the picture was unnerving, bringing back the memory of bodies laid thus by the contract surgeons' orderlies during the war. But this sensation, too, was momentary only. This was a time of astringent pleasure for a patrol commander. A tilted coffee-pot on a night-dead fire, saddles and *aparejos* humped on the ground, the sweet steam of new droppings along the horse-lines, woolly-bellied mules flicking their jack-rabbit ears. The picket-line sentry was stepping from man to man, prodding the dead blanket-rolls to life with the butt of his carbine, calling softly and musically, and quite unlike a white sentry who, Byrne knew, would awaken his comrades with obscene jests, anxious for them to relieve his loneliness. The sentry was Attucks, hat-brim back, suspenders white, and red undershirt showing below his cuffs, breeches tight on his great thighs. He made a rhythm and a song out of his gentle reveille. *'Get up, man, get up! And see the Lord's fine day!'*

Then suddenly the whole camp was awake, blankets heaving with the stretching of arms and legs, and this too was not like the rising of white troopers, men reluctantly abandoning the liberty of sleep and fortifying themselves with curses. These men came to life with a burst of happiness, singing and calling, joshing each other like children. As he walked down to the creek to freshen himself Byrne thought of what he had been told by other officers, that to command Negroes was an experience unmatched by anything else in the Army. A man, they said, had only to go about the coloured men's squad-fires at night to have depression driven from him. He could see the point, but he doubted whether innocent good-humour necessarily made a man a better soldier. A hard-swearing trooper with bone in his skull was the traditional objective of the drill-sergeants, and a man thus created might be expected to think sourly on the fact that he was selling his services for thirteen dollars a month, less twelve and a half cents deduction for the Soldiers' Home. Any soldier who came out of his dreams with pleasure might be reluctant to part with life altogether, which would mean he was no kind of soldier at all.

The argument was still unresolved in Byrne's mind when he returned to the bivouac. The troopers were grooming their horses as they ate their breakfast, and Nathan Donethegetaway was using the curry-comb on his own hair as well. Byrne looked at the horses with regret. He had a cavalryman's preference for one-colour troops, and these mounts were all colours, the bays, blacks, greys and sorrels unwanted by the other companies, and used to make Company M, last of all to be formed by the Tenth. It was inevitable that it should be known as the Calico Troop.

He studied his watch. The manual said that horses should be groomed for an hour and a half at least each morning, and the troopers were being faithful to the letter of the order, even on patrol. He wondered if this were Salem's idea, and he called the sergeant to him, ordering fires to be damped, the *aparejos* to be loaded on the mules and blinds to be set over the animals' eyes; he had had enough of their stubborn obstinacy yesterday. The valley air was now quite clear, and so still that a long-sighted man with time to spare might have amused himself by counting the leaves on the cottonwoods. The Comanches were already horsed, a knot of colour, and the women were perched like bundles of rags on the backs of the travois mules. Byrne sent Veal down the slope to discover what Quasia had in mind, and he was no wiser when the half-breed returned and said that the Comanches were thinking of asking the toad. What toad?

'Don't know, lieutenant, sir. Guess they want to make their medicine.'

Byrne sighed, and went his rounds, grumbling like a sergeant at a button unfastened, a quarter-strap twisted, a girth too tight. 'Damn it, man, you ought to know better. Slacken off and let the animal pass water in comfort!' Conception did so, his eyes widening at the torrential result.

The Comanches were moving, a line of them strung out one after the other, climbing the rise to the north-west, the men sitting like statues, with legs loose and backs bent, and here and there a feather sharp in shining hair. The sun caught the skin of them in gold and red, glinted on weapons, and glowed on mellow buckskin. The dog ran furiously, maddened with excitement, leaping, turning and twisting about the hooves. Quasia's yellow pony, draped with the scarlet blanket, had a power and grace that filled Byrne with envy.

There was nothing in Byrne's experience to guide him now, since the escorting of Indians on a buffalo hunt was not generally considered a field possibility, and he had a moment of indecision, the old familiar desire to leave responsibility to the rank above. Then he was amused by his situation, the sort of wry enjoyment one man might get from observing the difficulties of another, and this restored his self-reliance. He decided to begin, at least, by keeping the patrol in column, with right and left pointers out, half a mile to the rear of the Indians, closing the distance if the terrain gave them too much cover. He was aware that this showed his distrust of the Comanches, but it was wiser than thinking of them as Tatum did.

He mounted the patrol and waited until the Indians, who had gathered in a clump on the rise, made up their minds. Away to the rear of the patrol, behind the pack-mules, Honesty stood by his horse, his breeches bagging over his boots, his face sweating and his unhappy mouth slack. When Byrne walked his horse down the line, his thoughts protected by a frown, he did not look at Honesty, afraid that if he did so the sight of a cavalryman on foot would so offend his eye that he would order the boy to mount after all.

The Comanches moved down the other side of the rim, slowly, rider by rider until they disappeared. The poles of the travois kicked and jerked, the hide rolls bouncing in the triangles. Byrne raised his right arm. 'By twos ... Walk march, *ho!*' After twenty yards he gathered his horse to warn it of a change of gait, and thrust his fist into the air twice. The patrol went up the gentle slope at a reaching canter, forgetting Honesty who clawed his way in desperate pursuit. Topping the rise, Byrne saw that the Comanches had halted again, two hundred yards ahead, and that three of them had dismounted and were grubbing in the grass. 'Now what?' he said, but Veal did not know.

They watched, until one of the Indians cried out, raising his cupped hands. Byrne rode over. The man was holding a horned toad, his thumb clamped on its back to prevent it from leaping free. It was a comic and monstrous thing, five inches long, its oval back a fine yellow and purple. Its short tail jerked angrily and its brown-specked throat pumped with fear. The Indians were delighted with it, calling, and Quasia moved across to Byrne, placing a hand pleasantly on the lieutenant's shoulder. He nodded at the toad. '*Kusehtehmini!*' he said, and began to tap his head thoughtfully with a forefinger, a pedagogic gesture which, Byrne presumed, he had seen at the Pennsylvania Mission school and believed to be great medicine. But it did not help him to find the English for the word. Byrne looked at Veal.

Veal frowned, and for a moment seemed inclined to imitate the Comanche. Then he said, 'What they call the toad, lieutenant. Means asking him about buffalo.'

Byrne shrugged his shoulders and looked at the Indians with resignation. They had dismounted and gathered in a circle about the man with the toad. He placed it carefully on the ground, his hand blinding its eyes, and talked to it respectfully before he took the hand away. For a moment the toad remained where it was, its belly flat, legs outsplayed, ugly in shape, startlingly beautiful in colour. It changed front several times before setting off. The Indians parted to let it through, and watched until it disappeared. Quasia pointed to the west and looked at Byrne. 'Buffalo!'

'It seems to agree with the Caddoes,' said Byrne, 'or maybe they used the same toad.'

But no buffalo was found that day. The Indians moved at a walk, riding in a half-moon, and when, half an hour after leaving camp, Byrne halted to tighten girths, they would have dismounted and rested but for his angry protest. They smiled tolerantly and rode on. Sometimes they stopped abruptly, and remained motionless for minutes, staring to the west. When a raven flew over them, cawing harshly, they listened to its advice and nodded their heads. Perhaps, thought Byrne, this was more sensible than asking a toad for ravens liked to eat the bugs that lived on a buffalo's hide. He took what advantage he could from the frequent delays, ordering girths to be loosened and bits removed that the horses might graze.

He was profoundly bored. The land was empty yet full of noise, the rushing sea of the ceaseless wind about his ears, the soft fall of hooves, the song of leather and ringing canteens. The blue crescent of the Wichitas was to the north and east, but southward and westward rolled the tall grass, sweeping up the crests of low bluffs, and falling again in long surges. Before noon the sky to the north-west became dark, a deep petunia blue. The storm that broke was eight or ten miles away and the sound of it was like a distant battle. The troopers turned their faces towards it as they rode, watching with awe until the thunder died and a great rainbow arched. The clouds passed and the sky was once more a thin, hot, egg-shell blue. The violence and the beauty of what they had seen silenced the soldiers until Attucks, riding at the rear with the mules, began to speak, his voice rolling on rich chuckles. He mocked Honesty.

'Boy, you see that? You never seen nothing like that? Man, you know they get hailstones here like rocks?'

'That so?'

'That so. Big as the biggest melon you ever stole. How many melons you stole, Honesty, man?'

'Ain't figured.'

'You ought to know, boy. Man with a name like Honesty ought to know.'

'I told you. I ain't figured.'

'Why they call you Honesty, man?'

'It was my idea.'

'That so? Man, you sure put a load on yourself!'

At noon Byrne relieved the trooper from his trudging misery.

By the end of the day the patrol had ridden twenty miles to the west, parallel with the flow of the Red River and within another ten miles of the abandoned site of Camp Radziminski on the North Fork. Byrne reasoned that he could allow another day's ride westward which would bring them to the border of the Texas panhandle and the first rise of the High Plains. If buffalo were not found by then the hunt must turn back in a sweep toward Fort Sill, whatever Quasia intended. But he did not tell the Indian this. They camped that night by water where blue-stemmed grass was thick. Fires pricked the darkness, the wind fell and the smoke did not lift. The laughing, arguing voices of the troopers died one by one before Byrne himself slept.

Next morning they passed the rotting picket stockade of Radziminski and crossed the North Fork. The water was wide, shallow and bronze-coloured. The Comanches kept far ahead of the patrol, and seemed anxious to increase the distance. They rode in a bunch too, not in the lazy skirmish line of yesterday. This worried Byrne for an hour, and when he counted the Indians his uneasiness increased. He counted them again, and then again until there was no doubt in his mind that whereas there had been twelve of them the day before, men and women, there were now thirteen. He halted the patrol and fired two shots in the air from his pistol. The point men came back at the gallop.

The Comanche band shuddered when it heard the shots, but

it stopped. One rider on a brown and white pinto broke away, raced back towards the troopers for a hundred yards, turned his pony in narrowing circles, and returned. There was an angry calling and whooping.

'Veal!' said Byrne, and put his horse to a canter. When he came up with the Indians he saw the stranger immediately, a tall warrior, naked to the waist, and riding a light bay cavalry horse that had a small war-shield hanging on its flank. The man was painted and heavily armed with lance, bow, knife and carbine. He was a war-bonnet Indian, the feathers of the head-dress spilling in colour from a parfleche on the horse's croup. Byrne pointed to him. 'Who is he?'

Quasia smiled soothingly. 'My brother Ohanaki.'

'He's no agency Indian. Where's he from?'

Quasia looked at Veal and pointed to the west, speaking quickly, but Byrne did not wait for a translation. 'Quasia, I know what he wants. Send him away.'

The Comanche shook his head. 'Many buffalo,' he said, 'three four days. Ohanaki has seen them.'

'I know what he's seen. He's from Quanah and he wants you to join the hostiles. Send him away Quasia, and keep your honour.'

'Many buffalo.'

'Send him away.'

Quasia looked at Byrne coldly, and folded his hands on the neck of his horse. Byrne stood in the stirrups and waved his arm to the right and left and then brought it forward. There was a moment's silence before they heard the ring of metal and the gallop of hooves as the patrol came up in skirmishing line.

'Quasia, send your brother away.'

For a long time the young man looked at the officer impassively, while the other Indians began to move nervously. Ohanaki smiled, taking deep breaths that arched his chest, but when Quasia at last spoke to him his face darkened. He walked his horse up and down crying to the hunters, and when they showed no response, beyond unhappy glances at Quasia, he moved across to Byrne, reaching out with his lance. He tapped it lightly on the lieutenant's shoulder. 'A-he!' he shouted, counting coup. There was a sharp hiss of admiration and Quasia looked miserable, but he shook his head.

Ohanaki spat in his brother's face, pulled his horse about with a shout and galloped away to the west. Troopers and Indians watched him go until he was dissolved by the quivering heat. 'That was wisely done, Quasia,' said Byrne.

The Comanche shook his head. 'Many buffalo,' he said, and turned his back.

Two hours before dusk, where the land was broken by narrow draws that rain-fed the Salt Fork of the Red when there was water, but which were now bottomed with dry bunch-grass, the first buffalo sign was met. It was not a good sign, a cloud of buzzards in the air, climbing and falling like black flies on a blue wall. And then a foul and nauseous stench that pulled up the horses' heads wildly. The smell and the sight of the buzzards excited the Comanches, and they began to run their ponies across the grass in mad wheelings, calling angrily to the sky and the earth, moving faster and faster until they were more than a mile ahead of the patrol, and Byrne had to put the troopers to the gallop to decrease the gap.

They came over a rise to a wide saucer one thousand yards in diameter, and there the Comanches had halted silently. Byrne swore. Below, the grass was scattered with shining red hummocks, an obscene litter of flesh, and the air was full of the screeching, wing-flapping feasting of the birds, the phrenetic orchestration of insects. The stink of rotting, hideless meat forced vomit into Byrne's mouth, and he pulled his bandanna to the bridge of his nose. He had never before seen the wrack left behind by white hide-hunters, and he stared at it with appalled fascination. The bodies were grouped thickly at the bottom of the saucer, thinning towards the rim, and because they were close together he knew that the hunters, lying on their bellies downwind, with their rifles growing hot on the rests, had made an historic stand, killing and killing until the stupid beasts, maddened at last, broke out of the melée. He tried to count, but found this impossible because of the crawling quarrelling of the buzzards. Even so, he decided, there must be two hundred or more carcasses there, stripped of hides worth three or five dollars in Kansas. The flesh left for buzzards, wolves and ravens, the blood to feed lush grass, the bones to bleach. He was empty with shock, his exhausted breathing sucking in the wet bandanna.

The Comanche women began to keen, rocking their bodies on the wooden saddles, but the men sat in dejected silence, staring at the great slaughter. At last Quasia walked the yellow pony across to Byrne. Empty-eyed, he placed a hand on the lieutenant's wrist, and then pointed. 'Many buffalo!' he said. 'Why kill and not eat?'

They rode away.

The sun set quickly in a vermilion smear, but they continued to ride, southwards now, and in the moon that rose Byrne could see the white, bobbing buttocks of the Indians' ponies, the quirt-flailing arms, and he wondered how long the cavalry horses could stand this pace; what, if anything he could do if Quasia decided to ride all night until he reached the Red, cross it, and go raiding bitterly in Texas. Then, suddenly, the Indians halted and built their fires. There was no sound from them that night, and they played no games.

At noon camp next day Byrne was able to send word back to Sill. A rider came up from the south, a white trooper on a big black horse who hailed them from a mile away, waving his arm across his head before pitching down towards them at the gallop. He was a tall boy with spikes of yellow hair below the sweaty crown of his hat, and there was red dust on his face licked clear about his lips, and red mud caked on the breast and belly of the horse. He came into the camp and his pale blue eyes stared at the Negro troopers, and he reported himself as a private of the 7th riding up from Texas with despatches for Fort Sill. He looked again at the troopers who had gathered about him smiling. He looked down at them from his big horse, ignoring Byrne after that first casual report and salute, and he said, '*Niggers!*'

He said it easily in a rich molasses voice sliding insolently from the corner of an insolent smile. 'Nigger horse-soldiers,' he said, and laughed incredulously.

35

The smiles remained on the faces of the coloured troopers but the welcome went out of their eyes. Salem stepped forward and, in a voice remarkably empty of any feeling, said 'Mind your tongue, white man!'

The trooper looked at him, and then glanced at Byrne with the beginning of a wink. He said, 'And a high-yaller sergeant, too!' He dismounted and handed the reins to Salem. 'You hold my horse while me and the lieutenant talk.'

Byrne stared at the boy sickly. It was as if all the reasons why he should or should not do this or that raced crazily through his mind. He could not dress down the boy himself for that would be an inference that a coloured sergeant should not reprimand a white trooper. On the other hand, as he looked at Salem's tight face he knew that the sergeant was forcing the responsibility on to Byrne. Then it was too late, the white boy was pulling off his gauntlets and thrusting them into his belt, loping across to the coffee-pot and drinking from its spout. He spat the dust from his mouth, grinned cheerfully, and drank again.

Byrne turned away, his back to the stares of his patrol, and he sat on the ground fumbling for his glasses. He wrote his report, hearing the insolent whistle of the white trooper in the silence.

To Captain Henry Alvord,
Cdg Co. M. Tenth (Coloured) Cavalry,
Fort Sill, Ind. Terr.

Sir: My command is approximately five miles north of the Red River, south by west of Camp Radziminski. No buffalo have yet been killed by the Comanche but I have to report the following:

1) The party has been visited by an emissary from Quanah Parker's hostiles. I am satisfied that Eagle-Tail-Feather has no intention of agreeing to any suggestion made by this Indian but the temper of the hunting-party has been seriously affected by the fact that

2) Yesterday we found evidence of a great slaughter of buffalo by white hide-hunters who are apparently working in this region although ordered to remain north of the Arkansas River.

3) If we do not come up with the remainder of the herd within 24 hours I intend to return to the post.

G. A. Byrne, Lt.

He folded the report, stood up and handed it to the white trooper. The boy's face was peculiarly blurred, and Byrne blinked for some seconds before he realized that he was still wearing the spectacles. He removed them in embarrassment, and the blurred face resolved itself into an amused grin and mocking eyes. The youthful and self-possessed insolence of the trooper both alarmed and irritated Byrne. He thrust his hands into his waistband and tilted his head.

'Soldier,' he said, 'just now you called my men niggers and you insulted my sergeant.' He could see the troopers, out of earshot fifteen yards away, crouched on their heels and silent.

The boy's pale eyes widened in surprise. 'Hell, lieutenant. I ain't got nothing against black boys. My pappy owned three onetime, all bigger than them blue-gummed bucks you got here.'

Byrne was disarmed by the trooper's cheerful lack of understanding. He wished, for a moment, to be a sergeant again so that he might brow-beat the boy with parade-ground obscenity, and because of this there was a stilted solemnity in what he did say. 'Soldier, maybe you're not aware of it, but the Tenth Cavalry was formed by Act of Congress in July 1866 on the advice of General Sherman. Those aren't niggers, they're United States cavalrymen.'

The trooper looked at him, the white-lashed lid of one eye flickering, as if he were about to wink again. 'Yes sir, lieutenant. By the same Act of Congress I heard they formed the Seventh, only we ain't got no coloured gentlemen in that, so maybe I don't know how to talk about them.' He saw the flush on Byrne's face, and for the first time there was a faint uncertainty in his voice. 'No offence, lieutenant, but I see cavalrymen one way, and these just don't look like horse-soldiers to me.'

However reluctantly, in an oblique sense Byrne could understand the boy there. It had been the sight of a squadron of green-jacketed dragoons leaping a dry-stone wall in Galway (and he only ten at the time) that had filled him with admiration for the horse-soldier, and a terribly desperate desire to be one himself one day. He had never really understood why he should have admired those dragoons at that moment instead of hating them, for within the hour they were herding himself, his father, mother and four sisters down the road to Lough Corrib, and his father mad with whiskey and anger and hate, cursing the fine English officer who scarcely looked at them from above his auburn whiskers. They had slept the night in a ditch, and although he had heard his mother's sobs and his father's curses his mind had still been inflamed with the picture of those grand soldiers on their high black horses.

He shook the memory from his thoughts. 'Trooper, next time you see a coloured soldier remember he wears the same blue uniform as you and is entitled to the same respect. If we ever meet again, and I hear you talk out of the side of your mouth like this, I'll run you up to Sherman himself.'

The boy saluted. He was no longer smiling. He walked to his horse, and when he had climbed into the saddle he looked at the Negroes one by one, his eyes remaining longest on Salem. Then he struck the horse and rode across Byrne's front at the gallop. They could still hear his shout long after the falling ground to the north-east had hidden him.

Now all the troopers were looking at Byrne – Salem, Attucks, James, Conception, Nathan Donethegetaway, all of them, their eyes white and their hands hanging idle. They had not heard what he had said to the white boy, and Byrne resented the feeling that he should have made certain that they did. He knew that he had made a mistake again, but his annoyance was less with this than with the circumstances that pushed him into a conflict he did not want. What did they expect of him? He had no desire to fight their battle, and if they believed he had failed them what could he do about that? They were free, weren't they, and hadn't enough white men died to make them free? But he knew that he had made a mistake again.

'Mount up! Salem, get this damned patrol in the saddle!'

Two hours after noon one of the Indians who was riding far out on the right, three-quarters of a mile away on the long spine of a ridge, suddenly halted and began to gobble like a wild turkey. The Comanches drew together and moved towards him. Byrne put the patrol to the trot, and when it reached the ridge he saw the land dropping sharply to a shallow valley four or five miles in length, with dry sandy runs making lateral strokes on either side like the skeleton of a leaf. A mile and a half away was a small herd of fifteen buffalo cows, baked mud thick on their flanks, and reddish-yellow calves playing about them. The wind blew from them, smoothing the grass with ripples of silver, and bringing the rumbling of the cows' bellies. High over the heads of the patrol a meadow-lark climbed in golden song.

The Comanches were excited. They began to strip to the breech-clout. They took the blanket-pads or wooden saddles from their ponies, and some wound coils of grass rope just behind the forelegs, thrusting their knees beneath it when they mounted. Quasia looked at the sky and he looked at the buffalo and he spoke quickly, waving his arm to the left and to the right. While the others were armed with bow or gun, he carried a lance only, a shaft of bois d'arc seven feet long, a leaf-shaped iron head at one end and tufted feathers at the other. Byrne knew enough about Indians to recognize in this weapon a manifestation of Quasia's pride and honour, for the lance was the old way and the hard way of the Comanche buffalo-hunter.

Quasia raised his hand and lowered it quickly, and the Comanches began to walk their ponies down the valley in a half-moon, the horns of which grew further and further apart as they advanced. The buffalo were not alarmed. Their eyes, obscured by the mud-plastered hair, saw nothing, and they smelt nothing. In half an hour the crescent of Indians had almost encircled the herd, and it began to contract. Byrne watched tensely, admiring the graceful carriage of the men, the ponies stepping prettily.

The boom of a gun came unexpectedly, one shot from the top of a bluff a mile away, and a feather of white smoke clouding and then disappearing. The Indians halted, their heads turned. On the far side of the herd one of the cows went slowly down on her belly, her forelegs splayed, and even at this distance Byrne could see the black blood streaming from her nostrils. The others stopped and the smell of blood came to them. Two began to bellow, and the calves ran in, like pebbles sucked down a drain. Then, with heads down and tails stiffly up, the herd began to run, madly into the man-smell of the Comanches and then swerving from it, rocking at incredible speed, breaking the walls of the narrow draws as they crossed, the red calves long-legged in the rear. The earth vibrated with a drum-roll.

The Comanches, when they had recovered from their immobilizing surprise, whooped and kicked at their ponies, but the report of the gun and the smell of blood had scared the herd too soon. Only Quasia had skill enough and pony fast enough to carry him in for a kill. He rode to within a yard of the biggest cow, coming up on it from the right and behind, holding his lance in both hands with the point down. For a moment the red dust hid him, and then Byrne saw him strike, downward and forward, aiming for the heart with the thrust of both arms.

The jerk of the blow tore the lance from Quasia's hands. The cow stumbled, thrust its head into the earth and went over with legs kicking. The fallen animal and the triumphant Indian, his throat throbbing with a yell, were left alone on the floor of the valley as the herd went over the rise half a mile to Byrne's left. Quasia pulled the lance free and held it over his head.

Now Byrne remembered the shot, and he shouted to Attucks to take a trooper and ride over there. They went at the gallop, yelling, with buttocks lifted, brims of their hats blown back and their carbines flapping. They circled on the rim, standing in the stirrups to stare westward beneath their hands, and then one dismounted and knelt on the ground.

The whispering women passed Byrne on their way down to the dead buffalo, riding high on the mules, the yellow dog trailing in the dust of the travois poles. The warriors below had assembled in an angry knot, shouting and waving weapons, but Quasia remained alone by his kill, his retrieved lance in his hand and his head up. Byrne sighed and moved down the rise, telling Salem to keep the patrol ready.

Attucks and the trooper met him before he reached Quasia. 'Just a white man high-tailing, lieutenant, sir,' said the corporal. ' 'Bout a mile off.' He held up the brass shell-case of a ·50—70 buffalo gun.

'Damn the bastard!' And Byrne continued to swear until he was halted by the troopers' stares.

'Something else, sir,' said Attucks. 'Smoke. Maybe three, four miles thataway apiece.' He pointed to the south-west.

Byrne twirled his hat, and when the rest of the patrol came down, leather creaking and water sounding in the canteens, he told Salem to ride off and scout the smoke, without being seen if possible, and to report back as soon as he could. He ordered Attucks to loosen girths and unbit the horses, and he shook his head when Crispin asked if he should make coffee. 'Let the horses have water,' said Byrne, 'and each man one mouthful.'

He rode across to the Indians, wondering whether Quasia would consider the meat of two cows enough to maintain his reputation as a hunter, but doubting it. On his way he passed a wallow, churned into mud and fouled with droppings as he had expected, and he knew that whatever the Comanches intended they must move on and find water by dusk. Quasia ignored him, but whether in anger or in fierce elation Byrne could not tell. The young man's eyes were closed, his nostrils flaring, his lips moving soundlessly. The blood of the buffalo was on the arm that held the lance. Admiring the boy, Byrne nonetheless felt curiously lonely, as a man does when he is shut out from the emotions of another.

He turned to watch the women, already at work on the butchering. They were only girls, their bodies heavy-hipped, their skirts swinging and their bobbed hair blowing about their faces and masking the laughter in their eyes. Heaving and pulling, slipping on the bloody earth, they turned each buffalo over on its belly, its legs spread, making a mockery out of its shaggy dignity. The hide they slashed across the brisket at the neck, and when they had folded back the skin they removed the forequarters at the joint and placed them wetly on the grass. They worked quickly and efficiently. They cut along the spine to the tail, carefully removing the sinews before peeling back the hide on either side, exposing the creamy tallow and red flesh. Both were now smeared with blood, and flies gathered in black flowers on their arms and on the buffalo meat. They cut the flank up towards the stomach and removed it in one piece with the brisket, rolling up the whole like a blanket. They chewed strips of sinew noisily as they worked, and now and then they paused to kick away the dog.

The sweet smell of blood tightened the muscles in Byrne's face, but he watched with fascination. One woman cut through the belly wall and removed the entrails, and now the men came forward to help, first slicing the smoking liver with their knives and cramming it into their mouths. The pock-marked boy held up a strand to Byrne, and then offered him a string of gut, laughing and eating them himself with exaggerated pleasure when the lieutenant shook his head. The men pulled at the ribs one by one, the bones cracking, breaking them free until all that remained was the matted head. Some of the greater bones the Comanches cracked with their axes, thumbs scooping out the marrow. The blood seemed to make them drunk, for they began to sing, beating each other violently on the back.

Byrne rode to Quasia and touched the young man on the shoulder. 'We must find water,' he said. Quasia, too, was like a drunken man, and he did not reply. 'There'll be no more hunting,' said Byrne. 'Tomorrow we must return. Understood?'

The mist cleared from Quasia's eyes. He gestured violently to the west. 'Many buffalo,' he said, 'Many more.'

Byrne shook his head. 'No. My horses need forage.'

Quasia spoke angrily in his own tongue, striking his hands across his body at the waist, and the others came crowding about him, looking up to Byrne with blood on their lips. Then they began to argue among themselves, and he shrugged his shoulders and went back to the patrol, moving it upwind, away from the flies and the stench of meat.

When the sun was two handsbreadths above the horizon, and the Comanches sleeping in the shadows of their droop-necked ponies, Salem came in. They saw him first over a mile away, tall in the saddle, riding easily and steadily, his bleached

42

hat startlingly white. When he reached them he gave Byrne a perfunctory salute, his calm face challenging the little officer's thoughts. 'The smoke's from a homestead by an oxbow bend in a big river.'

'The Red?'

'I think so.'

'How far?'

'Three miles, maybe four.'

'Who's there?'

'I saw a white woman.'

'Did you speak to her?'

Salem smiled gently. 'No sir, the lieutenant told me not to be seen. And I figured that though she was only a woman she was white, and maybe with no kind thought for a poor coloured soldier.'

Byrne stared up at him bleakly. 'I don't like your sense of humour, sergeant.'

'Begging the lieutenant's pardon.'

'Did you ride over to the Texas side?'

'No, sir.'

'Well, sergeant,' said Byrne heavily, 'since you seem pretty chippy, you can ride on back there and scout the other bank. Rejoin us at the house.'

Salem saluted with a faint inclination of head and shoulders, turned his horse and walked it away to the south. His hands on hips and his brows frowning above his beaten nose, Byrne watched. *That was probably another mistake, damn your temper!*

They came to the Red River. The evening light lay on the copper water and the air was still. From a spur of high ground, looking across its skirt of scrub-oak, Byrne saw the homestead. It was a single-storey house built of sod-bricks neatly cut, a roof of wood and grass and earth on which wild flowers were growing in yellow clusters. The walls had been pierced for windows, but although there were frames there was no glass. There was a post-rail corral and a sad grey horse, an old Conestoga wagon-box with the wheels missing. Beside the tall green palisade of the corn-patch a turkey-hen moved among the chickens, a sow and her litter rooting.

Byrne halted the patrol, but the Indians moved on down through the scrub to the water. He called: 'Hallo, there, in the house!' When there was no reply he took the patrol down, ordering it to make camp a hundred yards from the river, where the grass thickened on the baked mud. Then he saw a flash of colour at a window of the house, and heard a door slam. He rode over with Attucks, and it was the corporal who first saw the barrel of a rifle moving across a lower rail of the corral. He pointed to it, the red flannel of his shirt pulling out beyond his cuff, and his breath whistling between his teeth. Byrne dismounted and walked casually towards the corral, slapping the dust from his thighs with his hat, and not lifting his head until he was two yards from the rail. At the end of the rifle was a brown face, a thick mat of sun-bleached hair. Child and man stared at each other.

'Well, boy,' said Byrne at last, 'are you going to fire?'

The boy stood up, the long rifle dragging, and he put his hand inside his shirt and scratched his chest. There was a rent in his jeans and a scab of blood on his knee. He looked about

44

ten years of age and he scowled truculently at Byrne. 'Ain't loaded, anyway,' he said. 'You scared, though?'

'Maybe.'

The boy pointed with a black-rimmed nail. 'Them real Indians, Mister?'

'Real Indians,' agreed Byrne. 'You're not alone here?'

The boy grinned, a gap-toothed breeching of his face, and now he began to scratch his hair. 'There's Maw and Jinny in the house. She's my sister. I'm the only man.'

'That explains the rifle. Call your mother.'

'What them Indians want down here?'

'I'll take you down to meet them later.'

'Will I need the gun? I got shells for it.'

'No, they're peaceful.'

'Then what they got soldiers with them for?'

'Call your mother, boy.'

The boy grinned again. 'She's scared. She thinks I'm in the hide-hole only I ain't. She only saw the Indians. Sure I won't need the gun?'

'Come here, boy,' said Byrne. He leant over the rail, lifting the child by the shoulders and placing him down outside the corral. 'Get along to your mother!' He beat his hand against the seat of the boy's breeches to set him off, but before the child reached the house the door opened and a woman came out.

'*Davy!*' she cried, going down to clutch the boy, her skirt billowing. And she looked up to Byrne.

He saluted and took off his hat. 'Ma'am. I'm sorry if we frightened you.'

'I saw Indians.'

'It's a hunting party from the agency.'

She arose and looked at him intently, frowning as if she did not understand, and her eyes passed from him to Attucks, her hand moving protectively to her side, and Byrne saw that there was another child there behind the woman's skirts, a girl with yellow hair like the boy, and the same blue eyes. The child looked at him shyly and then pressed her face against her mother.

The woman placed her hand over her eyes, against the red

45

set of the sun, staring at the troopers. 'I'm sorry,' she said, as if she believed her alarm had offended him. 'We've been alone too long.'

'There's no man here?'

'My brother's gone down into Texas. My man died six months ago from a sickness.' He followed her stare, and saw the mound on a slope beyond the corn-patch, the case-plank cross weathered white. She was still confused and she looked back to the troopers. 'So many men,' she said, and laughed quickly. 'Ain't seen so many men in a long time.'

She pushed a hand at her hair. She was a young woman, taller than Byrne and straight-backed. Her shoulders were broad and she carried her head well on her neck. Her face was thin, but well-boned. 'My name's Anne Norvall . . .'

'Byrne,' he said.

'You'll want coffee, maybe.' She turned towards the house and then turned back, looking at Attucks. 'Perhaps your men . . . Are they all coloured?'

'All of them, ma'am,' he said stiffly. 'We are a patrol from the Tenth.'

She sensed his resentment. 'I didn't mean what you think.'

'No, ma'am.'

'It's just if they want anything. Sweetening, maybe. I've got molasses. I've heard coloured people like molasses.'

'We can't take things you'll need, ma'am.'

'There's enough of it,' she said a little bitterly, 'and to spare.' She bent and whispered in the boy's ear, and, with a backward grin at Byrne, he ran into the house.

'Will you step inside, you're welcome!' she said, and now that the tension had passed from her face he saw that her mouth was full and her smile serene. 'I'd be happy to have you sleep here. There's bacon, and we've got eggs.' Her eyes strayed to the Indian camp and the mouth tightened again.

'There's nothing to fear from them,' he said gently, 'but I'll put a sentry on the house tonight, if you wish.'

'There's no call. But it's strange . . .'

'I promised the boy I would take him down to them. But if it's not to your liking . . .'

46

Davy had returned with a jar, and she put a hand on his head, ruffling his hair affectionately. 'He'd sneak down anyway. Will you have coffee now?'

'No,' he said, 'thank you. I'd like to come back this evening if I may.' The girl Jinny was smiling at him from the folds of her mother's skirt, and he smiled back at her. 'Don't be afraid of the Indians,' he said.

'We won't,' she said, and smiled again. He watched her return to the house. She had a way of holding her skirt by one hand that pleased him, as did the straight-backed courage of her walk.

Salem came over the river. His face was weary and his uniform white with dust. He reported without emotion. He had scouted along the Texas bank for three miles, he said, and he had found the cold ashes of a fire, the marks of many shod horses that had been picketed in something like a cavalry line. He had no explanation to offer, and Byrne did not ask for one, but told Salem to put a sentry in close to the house, with orders to call if the Indians wandered that way. The rest of the troopers he sent down to bathe, out of sight of the homestead.

He went down to the water himself, stripping naked and walking into it, feeling the cold rise over his knees and contract the muscles of his stomach. Then he held his nose and sat on the river bed, coming up with a great splutter and shaking the water from his lank hair. When he had soaped himself, and immersed himself again, he walked out to where Crispin had laid a towel and a razor. Still naked, he shaved himself, watching the troopers.

They played like children, flipping their big hands along the surface of the water. Only Attucks seemed able to swim, turning and diving like a seal, his black skin shining on his superb muscles, staying below the water for a long time and coming up to release the last air from his lungs with a great shout of delight. He mocked the others, Riddle particularly. The stunted, puff-cheeked trumpeter walked splay-footed in the shallows, wearing his stringy nakedness with dignity as if it were his uniform, chewing tobacco still and spitting yellow streams each time Attucks called to him.

The trooper Salvation Calhoun did not play and joke, but stood apart in the water surlily, and because of this Byrne watched him uneasily. His skin was almost as pale as Salem's, but whereas the sergeant's face was calm and distant Calhoun's was hot and angry with some inner resentment. Not only did he refuse to join the others in their joshing, Byrne saw, but they seemed to ignore him.

They ignored Nathan Donethegetaway, too, although this was obviously in respect. The old man stood with his back to them, bending, ritually almost, to cup his hands below the water and pour it over his head. In the thickening dusk his grey hair was now white, his fragile body supported on the bent sticks of his legs. Now and then he changed position, walking to cleaner, unmuddied water, his big head nodding gently on his neck. His back was corrugated by the scars of old whiplashes.

When first he saw these scars Byrne was shocked, and something of his surprise and horror must have been reflected in his face, for when he at last looked away from the old man he saw Salem smiling at him ironically. It was almost as if the sergeant were proud of those scars on Nathan's back.

An hour after dusk the boy Davy came into their camp. His face had been scrubbed, his hair slicked back, the rent in his jeans sewn up, and he carried an armful of corn-meal bread which he laid by the fire. He looked at Byrne and said, 'You ain't forgotten, Mister?'

Byrne had not forgotten, but he was now regretting his promise. There had been no movement from the Indian camp. The glow of their fire broke in fragments across the river water, and he could hear the murmur of their voices, smell the meat roasting. He wondered if Quasia, embittered perhaps by the loss of the herd, would welcome visitors.

'You ain't forgotten?'

'No,' said Byrne, 'I haven't forgotten. Take my hand, boy.'

They heard a cry from the Indians before they reached the fire and they saw Quasia standing up, the scarlet blanket slipping from his shoulders to his hips. A rough scaffolding beyond the fire gleamed red where the women had hung the buffalo fillets, sliced thinly for drying in the sun, and Byrne looked at this sourly, knowing that it meant the Indians proposed to camp here for two days at least. Buffalo hump ribs leant like arches over the roasting-fire.

'Davy,' said Byrne slowly, so that his words might be understood by the Indian, 'this is Quasia. He is a Kwahadi Comanche and a great hunter of buffalo.'

Quasia bent down to stare at Davy, his cheeks shining with the grease of the meat he had been eating. The boy's fingers tightened on Byrne's hand, but he made no other movement. Quasia wiped a hand on his leggings and held it out. 'OurFather whichartinheaven,' he said.

'Hallowed be Thy name!' shouted Davy in delight, and he released Byrne's hand and grasped Quasia's.

The Indian smiled. Still holding Davy's hand he turned to the fire and spoke, resting his other fingers on the boy's yellow hair.

'Is he going to scalp me, Mister?'

'No, boy. It's just that he's never seen hair the colour of yours.'

Quasia led Davy to the fire, kicking the dog from his way with a sweep of his foot. He sat down and gently pulled the boy on the blanket beside him, and he leant forward, tearing a rib from the fire and thrusting it into the child's hand.

'It's hot,' said Davy.

'Eat,' said Quasia. 'Look!' And he bit into the meat himself. 'Eat it, boy. Have you never eaten buffalo rib?'

'No, Mister Byrne, sir, but Maw said I gotta eat nothing they gave me.'

'You eat, boy. I'll explain to your mother.'

Byrne was still standing behind them, and Quasia looked upwards over his shoulder, staring at the lieutenant for some seconds. Then he pointed to a place on the other side of the boy and turned his face back to the fire. Byrne sat with legs crossed and took the rib offered him. He saw the grease-shining faces about the fire, and the sparks spinning upward, heard the crack and spit of roasting meat, the smack of lips and the belching, the fast run of the river, the hum of cicadas, and the gentle singing of one of the women as she beat on a parfleche.

The taste of the meat was rich in his mouth and a feeling of pleasure strong inside him.

When he had finished the rib Quasia threw the bone over his shoulder and wiped his fingers carefully on his leggings. He touched the boy's ear and then held up a finger to command the child's attention. He began to identify some of the men about the fire, saying first their Comanche name and then giving it a rough English translation. With some surprise Byrne realized that until this moment only Quasia had seemed an individual to him, the others had been part of a fabric woven in harsh colours against the sky or the prairie grass. They were all young men, and when their names were called by Quasia they inclined their heads briefly and in respect.

Pakawa – Kills-Something – was the round-faced young man who was running to fat. His dark eyes glittered like berries in his pock-marked cheeks. The grin that remained fixed on his lips was unnerving, and when his name was called he punched his stomach and mocked his grossness.

Ekakura – Red-Buffalo – was tall for a Comanche and narrow-chested, his hair a dark brown rather than black. Somewhere in his lineage, Byrne thought, had been a white woman, taken captive in one of the old Kwahadi raids down to the Brazos and the Trinity. He was a dandy, his buckskin leggings ornamented with blue and white quills, and the soft breast feathers of a mallard were woven into the plaits of his hair. About his throat he had hung the brass gorget of a Mexican dragoon. He did not smile at Davy, and scarcely nodded. His face was inexorable, bitter and unforgiving.

Pinedapon – Whip-Owner – was almost a boy. He was perhaps sixteen, close enough in age to Davy to make a point of showing how unimportant this was. He sneered with a great curling of his upper lip, holding his head so stiffly on his neck that the three-feather cluster quivered in his hair. Quasia shook his head and spoke gravely to him, and the others laughed, and the arrogance went out of Whip-Owner's face, washed away by a warm smile.

Wepitapuni – War-Axe – was the oldest of them all. Thirty perhaps, thought Byrne. His chest and arms were scarred and he looked more like a Northern Cheyenne or Sioux than a Comanche. Quasia seemed to have a great affection for him, for he repeated the man's name several times, with increasing gentleness, reaching out an arm and locking it about Wepitapuni's shoulders. War-Axe nodded his head gravely to the white boy.

These four only did Quasia introduce by name, the others he indicated with a sweep of his hand. Byrne thought that they were perhaps his council, that any one of them could take his place as leader, and that he depended on their guidance as much as he did upon his own skill and wits. When he had finished the introductions Quasia was silent, staring at the fire and seemingly searching for words to say what was in his mind. At last he touched Davy's shoulder, touched his own eyes and let his hand move out from his face until the fingers were pointing at the fillets of meat on the scaffolding. 'Buffalo!' he said, and he pointed to the robe on which War-Axe sat, saying 'Buffalo!' again. He touched the water-bag and said 'Buffalo!', the chips of the fire and said 'Buffalo!' Again and again he identified things with the same word, his voice lifting, and Byrne realized that Quasia was no longer talking to Davy alone but to him, and through him to other white men, affirming his people's desperate dependence on the animal.

Then he was silent again, thinking, and when at last he began to speak, in English, he held Davy's hand, smiling down at him paternally. Byrne was moved, as much by the affection in Quasia's face as by the story he was telling, sometimes in verbless, halting sentences, sometimes in words of powerful emphasis, but slowly, very slowly as he dragged them from his memory.

The other Indians, understanding nothing, nonetheless sensed the importance of the story. They sat erect, their hands loose between their knees, and their eyes on the fire.

The earth was made and so were The People, but the buffalo was not known. One day an old man came to where The People lived and watched the young men playing the wheel game. He stood with his quiver on his shoulder. Then he put the quiver down on the ground and said that he was going into the bushes to relieve himself. When he was gone The People looked into his quiver and saw that it was full of fat meat such as they had never seen before. Day after day the stranger came to watch the wheel game, and when they could The People looked into his quiver, and saw that it was always full of the fat meat. They were hungry, but the old man offered them none of the meat. So they asked the Owl to find out where he got the meat. The Owl flew over the mountain and perched on the poles of the old man's lodge. He saw the stranger and his wife and their daughter inside the tipi eating fat meat, and he flew back and told The People. They moved their village over the mountain, and when the stranger saw them he was angry and threatened them, saying they should come no closer. They waited, wondering how they could get some of the meat which the old man kept to himself greedily. At last a young medicine man said he would find out. He changed himself into a young dog, and when the old man was away from the lodge he crept up to it whining. The daughter took pity on him and opened the door of the tipi. He went in and he saw a great hole in the ground. He looked through the hole and saw a wide plain below, and the plain was covered by many, many buffalo. He thought of a clever idea, and he began to bark and shout through the hole until the buffalo became nervous and began to run. They ran up through the hole in the earth and smashed down the old man's tipi, covering the earth from sky to sky. That was how The People got the buffalo.

When Quasia had finished the story he was exhausted, his eyes heavy and his head bent, as if the effort of finding strange words to fit a familiar legend had been too much for him. Davy's face was red with the heat of the fire.

No one spoke until Byrne took the child's hand. 'Come on, boy,' he said, but Davy did not move. Byrne arose and picked up the child in his arms, and Davy went to sleep immediately, his mouth slack and his forehead pressed into Byrne's shoulder. The lieutenant had walked a hundred yards perhaps, and could plainly see the blanket rolls of the patrol, the glint of moonlight on the sentry's carbine, when he heard the soft whisper of moccasins on the grass. He stopped and turned.

It was Quasia. The Comanche looked at the boy and then at Byrne. He rested his hand momentarily on the officer's shoulder and nodded towards the house. They walked together, and when Anne Norvall met them, her eyes frowning at the Indian, he put his hand on the sleeping boy's head and smiled.

The dawn awakening, and eyes opening emptily to the sky. But there was Veal standing above him, and wiping his mouth nervously with the red bandanna. He said that two of the Comanches were missing, Whip-Owner and an older warrior called Brown-Young-Man. They had seen deer in the breaks across the Red, at first light when the mist was thick, and they had swum across with their bows to kill it. Byrne swore, and pulled on his boots, kicking at the dust as he walked down to the Comanche camp, his face flushed and his lower lip jutting. Quasia greeted him pleasantly, but seemed faintly disgusted by the lieutenant's anger, and when he was told what had caused it he cut his hand sharply across his chest and said, in his own tongue, that he would talk about the matter when Byrne had controlled himself.

Although resenting the rebuke the lieutenant was reasonable enough to appreciate its justice, and he stood for some seconds slapping his gauntlets on his thigh until he was calmer. Quasia took no advantage from the situation. He invited Byrne to sit, and offered him a cigarette. The air was still cold and the sun glittered in what was left of the mist. Quasia shivered a little beneath his blanket as he carefully returned to their buckskin bag the hair-pluckers he had been using. He then picked up a green stick, crushed the end into short strands with the flat of his knife, and began to clean his teeth. He inclined his head to indicate that he was ready to talk.

Answering Byrne's questions in his own tongue he said that the two men had gone across the river without his permission. For this they would of course be reprimanded by the police-men, Kills-Something and Red-Buffalo. They should not have gone, he admitted that, but he could not see that the matter

54

was as serious as Byrne's anger implied. For generations the great hunting ranges of Comancheria had stretched far south, across the Great River and into Mexico. Whip-Owner and Brown-Young-Man had listened to their fathers' tales and they were ambitious. But they would be punished. Quasia did not wish to quarrel with Byrne. He spat the threads of wood from his mouth and dropped the stick into the fire. Was the yellow-haired boy coming to see his friend this morning?

Byrne accepted the situation. He could scarcely do anything else. He was beginning to respect as well as like Quasia. The young man was a diplomatist. His reference to the wide spread of Comancheria in his father's day was a gentle reminder of how much the white men had taken from the Comanches, and how bitterly some of the Indians felt about this. His promise to punish Whip-Owner and Brown-Young-Man had been made in a spirit of conciliation, but it carried the suggestion that they would be punished as much for failing to ask Quasia's permission as for disobeying Byrne.

The lieutenant nodded, and he smoked silently before putting his next question. He had seen the drying-racks. If the Comanches intended to camp here for some time he could not permit it.

Quasia unbraided his hair and began to comb it, shamelessly admiring its length and sheen. Why? he said. It was the custom. If the soldiers could not feed their horses on summer grass like the Indian ponies that was surely no reason for interfering with the custom.

The soldiers were obeying orders, and The People must also obey orders now they had taken the white man's road. They must return to the agency today.

No, said Quasia. Tomorrow, perhaps. Tomorrow more buffalo might be found if the white hunters had not driven all the herds far on to the Staked Plains. As for the white man's road, not all Indians could be expected to ride along it at the same speed.

Byrne sighed, and threw the butt of the cigarette into the fire. Tomorrow then, he said.

Quasia smiled. Was the yellow-haired boy coming? he asked again.

Byrne nodded, and went back to the bivouac. He knew that he would have to inform Alvord of the situation, he could not rely on the chance of meeting another courier riding to Sill. He called Attucks and told him that he was sending him back to the post. At first the big Negro looked disappointed, and then the distinction of the duty came to him and a grin split his blue face. His spectacles slipping on his nose, Byrne wrote the report, the script sprawling across the page angrily. He hoped that Alvord, that Virginian manual-soldier, would have the intuition to understand.

To Captain Henry Alvord,
Cdg Company M,
Regt H.Q. Tenth (Coloured) Cavalry,
Fort Sill, Ind. Terr.

Sir: As implied by my last report to you I am using my discretion to extend the duration of this patrol for the following reasons:

1) Although we found buffalo yesterday the kill was disturbed by a white hunter and only two animals were killed.

2) The Indians insist on time for drying the meat.

3) I have assessed the situation and am confident that cautious use of forage and rations will make our return by Saturday feasible. It is hoped we may meet with more buffalo on our return, but I consider this unlikely. The illegal operations of white hunters in this territory have seriously affected the numbers of buffalo.

G. A. Byrne, Lt
Norvall's Crossing, I.T.

When Attucks had gone Byrne ordered a horse-inspection. The animals were in better condition than he had expected, and he realized, with a little shame, that this was because he had under-estimated the Negroes. He told Salem to see that the hooves were stuffed with wet clay. Two of the mounts needed a purge, and he wondered whether the woman would have the makings of a bran-mash. This, at least, was the excuse he gave himself for calling on her.

She seemed to be expecting him, opening the door of the house as he came by the corral. She was wearing a blue apron over her brown woollen dress, the skirts of which, lifted from the earth, showed her white stockings and heavy shoes. Her straight fair hair was parted in the middle, tied in a bun at the nape of her neck, and because it shone this morning he knew that she had been brushing it, and he wondered at this vanity in a frontier woman. He stood before her, his hat in his hand, and smiling. Jinny came out from behind her mother and surprised him by lifting her face to be kissed, her eyes closed. He picked her up and held her high above his head, laughing. And when he put her down the girl knotted her fist in the piping of his breeches.

Anne Norvall's face was warm with pleasure, and her smile smoothed the weather-etched lines at the corners of her eyes. She said, 'Davy went after breakfast. He went down to the Indians.'

'He'll be all right. Quasia likes him.'

'He's not a wild boy. But there's been no excitement like this. Not since the trail-herds stopped coming over. Will you come in, Mr Byrne?' She stepped aside, and as he passed her he caught the strong scent of soap, not perfumed, but something clean and wholesome. The house smelt clean and fresh too, with a sting of dust in the air that indicated she had recently swept the earth floor. There was only one room, divided at one end by a gunny-sack curtain neatly sewn. At the other end were shelves full of canned goods and jars. The coal-oil lamp had a wide shade with a frill of glass tears, and on the wall above it was a picture of a man in uniform, an infantry bugle on his cap.

She said, 'That was my man. He built this after the war when the Texas herds started going north. We were going to sell them supplies, but they started going over further east at Doan's Store, and there ain't been a herd through here since last year.' She said this in a level tone, without bitterness and without resignation.

'We could use supplies,' he said, 'I can give you a note against them. We could use oats.'

'There's some,' she said, 'there's some but I guess it may be spoiling. You could have a look at it.' And then she faced him, her hands clasped loosely over her apron, her head tilted a little to one side. 'You're old for a lieutenant,' she said abruptly, and then flushed. 'That ain't what I should say, is it?'

He smiled. 'I was a sergeant. It was a way of getting officers for the coloured regiments.'

'I like the way you smile. Seems you don't do it often, but when you do you mean it.' She saw the surprise in his face. 'I guess I shouldn't have said that either. When you live alone you get to saying what you're thinking out loud.' He admired the way she held up her head when she said this.

'It was kind of you to think it, and to say it.'

'I figure it's a fine thing to be, Mister Byrne, commanding coloured soldiers and all.'

'Yes,' he said, 'I suppose you could look at it that way.'

'Sit up,' she said, 'I got coffee on, and hot biscuits.'

He sat at the table, his back straight, his knees together and hands on his thighs, until the child Jinny climbed on to him and sat there with her thumb in her mouth and her eyes staring gravely into his face.

'It's a lonely life for you here,' he said.

'It is, I guess. But there's Davy, and there's Reuben his uncle. But my brother, that's Reuben, he's away down in Texas, figuring on finding some land down there. He wants us all to go south.' She brought coffee and, without asking him, put a spoonful of molasses in it. Then she sat opposite him, erect in her chair, holding her head up in that way he was liking more and more.

'You ain't American born, Mister Byrne?'

'No,' he said, 'you're right. I'm not.' The child had now curled herself against him, her head in the pit of his shoulder, and she was singing to herself softly, her fingers playing with the buttons of his blouse. The woman smiled with love, putting out a hand to brush back the hair from the girl's eyes.

'It's a big country. I guess you came because of that.'

'In a way,' he said. 'My father came because it was free. He was a tenant farmer in Galway.'

'That's some town in England?'

'It's in Ireland. It's not a town. A county. We were evicted when I was ten.' He saw her frown. 'They wanted the land and we had to go. Like they clear the Indians out here.' He had never thought of it like that before, and wondered why he should now, and whether the comparison was in fact true. 'I remember very little of it.' But he remembered the fine dragoons leaping the dry-stone wall, their sabres ringing as they came down. 'My father would talk about freedom the way another man might talk about drink.'

'That's hard to understand,' she said.

'Not if you know how he hated. He had six hundred years of hate behind him, and he lived on it, hating the landlords and the old ascendancy and the English at the back of them. He had to go on hating even when he came here, joining the Fenian Brotherhood.'

'That's some kind of church maybe?'

'It called for the same sort of faith. It wasn't enough for my father to have got away from the English, he wanted to hit at them, and the Fenian Brotherhood was going to invade Canada, but my father was dead before they got around to trying it.'

'I guess you hate too, Mister Byrne.'

He remembered that Tatum had asked much the same question, one that seemed to leave him naked. 'No ma'am,' he said.

'Not even Indians?'

'No,' he said in surprise.

'Most folk hate them, specially over the Texas side. Once the Rangers came over the river here. They said they were looking for a white girl the Comanches had taken. They said they'd been hunting for three months and they talked like it was hunting lion. I admired them, being so set on it and all. Then one of them showed me a belt he said he'd made out of a squaw's skin, said it was softer than a deer's. He wanted to give me the belt.'

Byrne cursed to himself and stroked the child's hair.

'He meant it well,' said the woman. 'You haven't eaten the biscuit.'

He took it, crumbling it in his fingers, putting the pieces into his mouth clumsily. 'You're a good cook, ma'am.'

'Davy told me the story the Indian told him. About the buffalo. Did you know it?'

'No,' he said. 'Quasia wanted him to understand what the buffalo means to the Comanche. Without it they may starve.'

'Will they?'

'I suppose so. They need not. There are Quakers at the agency who want them to grow beans and breed cattle.' His thoughts took a sudden and contrary twist, and he spoke them aloud almost unconsciously. 'The Comanches do well, considering. I never ate meat until we came to America. We had potato and onion stew. Then there were no onions, and in the year of the eviction there were scarcely enough potatoes. That was why my father hated, not enough potatoes.'

'You figure you and the Indians got treated the same?'

'Not the same,' he said, and smiled. 'The English never made belts from our skins.'

She spoke with a prim disapproval that reminded him of Tatum again. 'It ain't right to joke about it.'

'It was not meant as a joke,' he said, 'but to smile at some things that are past is one good way of living with the memory of them.'

'I don't understand that.' She fidgeted with the pleating of her skirt, folding it and pressing it between the palms of her hands. 'I'm afraid of them.'

'The Comanches? There's no need.'

'Once, when my man was alive that is, a party of them stopped by here. They came over the river. They had a white woman with them. They pulled her along on a rope, tied to a horse, and she kept falling down in the dirt. You could see she was white by the colour of her hair.' Her hand went instinctively to her own. 'My man stood them off with his gun and said he'd shoot them, and they went away. When they had gone he started crying on account of he hadn't been able to do anything for the woman.' When he said nothing she went on harshly, 'When I think of that I don't feel so bad about that Ranger with the belt.'

'No, ma'am.'

'Sometimes', she said, 'I think of going east, and living on a street, and maybe talking with other women, and a school for Davy and Jinny. Reuben says we could get those things down in San Anton' or Brownsville. A woman thinks about time passing, sometimes. She thinks about the times when she was pretty and all.' There was no embarrassment in her voice, it was as if she were talking to herself rather than to Byrne.

He took his watch from his pocket and looked at it, and he put the child gently on the floor. She held up her face with her eyes closed again, and he kissed her softly. Then he stood up.

'Thank you for your kindness, ma'am.'

'It's been good to talk. You'll come again maybe?'

'Yes,' he said, 'I'd like that.'

'There are things I'd like to know,' she said. 'Woman's things, if you'd take no offence at my asking. Just talk about the ladies at the fort.'

'I'd enjoy that.'

'Maybe,' she said, 'you'd have heard your wife talking of them, clothes and such.'

'I have no wife. But I'll try to remember what I can.'

She stood at the door watching him as he walked towards the bivouac, and she frowned a little, as if she were trying to understand some paradox in him, and as if the appearance of him puzzled her, his stocky body thrusting itself forward obstinately.

He was thinking that he was a fool, for many reasons, but most immediately for not telling her that there were no women at Sill and that he knew nothing of the things she wanted to know. He was faintly alarmed. He had not spoken of his father for many years, and never so frankly. It had been the talk of hate, hate that had destroyed his father as easily as drink, and the implicit suggestion in her conversation as much as in Tatum's that a man must have hate in him somewhere, like original sin.

He went to find the boy, to send him back to his mother. The child was by the fire and Quasia was telling him another story.

Byrne halted behind them, aware that neither the boy nor the man knew he was there.

The Great Spirit made The People from the earth. From what he had already made. Thus he took the dust ...

(Quasia took earth in his fingers, held it level with his face, and let it dribble through them)

... and from this he made the flesh of The People. He took white stones from among the grass ...

(Quasia held one between thumb and forefinger, turning it slowly)

... and from these he made their bones. The blood of The People he made from the dew. The eyes of The People were made from the deep pools and filled with the light of the sun. He blew the wind into the lungs of The People and strengthened their arms with storms. He gave their faces his own beauty and made their thoughts from waterfalls. When he was finished The People were giants. Their heads were in the clouds and they could see from one end of the earth to the other.

'You ain't that big now,' said Davy.

Quasia shook his head. Work and bad food, he said, had reduced The People to their present stature. He saw Byrne and smiled to him pleasantly.

'Boy,' said the lieutenant, 'get along home to your mother. She's fretting about you.' He watched the child running, the little legs pumping, and the fingers firing at imaginary dangers in the grass, and then he turned to Quasia. 'Where are the young men? Are they back?'

The Comanche looked across the river and shook his head. His smooth face was serene, but his eyes were concerned. Byrne sat beside him, offering him a cheroot. Quasia lit it from the fire, and when he had taken a mouthful of smoke he opened his lips and rolled it on his tongue.

'They've been gone too long, Quasia.'

The young man allowed the smoke to roll down the fluting of his tongue, and he nodded.

'You know I wish to be your friend, Quasia, and I speak for your own good. The Texans are angry about the raids your people make into their country.'

'It was our country,' said Quasia.

'It's not your country now. That's been agreed.'

Quasia closed his mouth and blew the rest of the smoke through his nostrils. 'You are friend,' he admitted, but he leant forward and tapped the shoulder-straps on Byrne's blouse. 'No friend,' he said.

'But for us,' said Byrne irritably, 'the Texans would come across the river and make vengeance raids on you, just as some of your people do in Texas.' But when the Comanche said nothing he stood up, dusting his trousers. 'You must be ready to leave in the morning, and I hope the young men have come back by then.'

Early in the afternoon there were shots from across the river, three of them, the first followed some seconds later by two others so close together to be almost one sound. Byrne hailed the sentry on the rise. This was Calhoun, and he answered surlily. He could see nothing. The land was all puckered like a toad's back over there, he said, and he could see nothing. Byrne ordered Salem to bring up the men from the river, where some of them had been washing their shirts, and he placed them in a skirmish line on foot, two hundred yards from the water. He looked anxiously at the Comanche camp. The Indians were all on their feet, gathered in a group and staring across the river.

Byrne walked down with Veal. The opposite bank was silent and deserted, and he heard the humming wings of a dragon-fly as it scouted the shallows at his feet. The sun was harsh on the yellow grass across there, turning a clump of trees into black, crouching animals, like buffalo seen against the morning light. He waited for half an hour, his back straight, his legs astride, his hands thrust into his waist-band, and he heard no more sound, no more shots. Once he glanced at the house, and he saw that Anne Norvall was at the door, her hands resting on the shoulders of her children, and he sent Salem across to her with the request that she go inside the house and stay there.

Then, from a fold in the ground opposite, a man came running for the river. He was an Indian and he was naked but for the clout, the braids of his hair swinging and the sun shining on sweat and grease. He ran straight for the ford, leaping into the water, raising his knees, bouncing from one yellow splash to another. Midstream, he called, and whatever he said burst open the clump of Comanches like a grenade. They ran to their ponies, pulling themselves up by the manes, and with weapons waving they rode down to the river.

'*Quasia!*' shouted Byrne, and he ran along the bank.

Whip-Owner came out of the water, his mouth open, his chest arching and collapsing. There was blood on his right arm. He came out of the water towards Quasia and fell on his face. He laid his cheek against the earth, his back jerking like a fish, and the Indians watched him stonily until he dragged himself to his hands and knees, and finally to his feet. A torrent of words, violent and exclamatory, cut and slashed by the movement of his hands, poured from his mouth.

'Veal?' said Byrne.

'It ain't easy, lieutenant . . .'

'Damn it, man, I don't want any poetry, just the facts!'

'He and the other got hit by white folk over there. They killed the other one, he says.'

Quasia dismounted and walked to Byrne with his head up. He made the killing sign with his hand.

'Lieutenant, sir . . .' said Veal nervously.

At that moment one of the Indians shouted, pointing across the river. Down to the water's edge on the far bank rode three white men. Then more, and then more, until there were perhaps thirty-five of them. They rode in loose military formation, in twos, although they appeared to be civilians. When they halted a long call came from them but the words were blurred. The two Indian women began to run up the rise, scrabbling on their hands and knees.

'*Tejanos!*' said Quasia softly. Even he seemed afraid.

'Veal,' said Byrne, slowly enough for Quasia to understand. 'Tell them I want no trouble with the Texans. Tell them to get over the rise out of sight and stay there.' He was surprised when the Comanches went without argument.

He walked up to the line of skirmishers, looking at them doubtfully. James and Conception had had no time to put on their blouses, and their breeches sagged below their bellies, their faces shadowed by their hats. All of them were holding their carbines across their chests and staring white-eyed across the river. He saw that they were afraid, and he felt that there must be something he could say to them if only he knew what. Only Salem and the trumpeter Riddle had ever fired at men before. The rest had never fired at anything more than the butts, and maybe not even those. He turned his back to them and looked across the river. The horsemen were still standing there, facing the north bank in line. They were all well armed. He saw the booted rifles, the cartridge belts and holstered pistols, the broad slant of low-crowned hats, and he knew what they were.

'Riddle, sound a call.'

'What call, lieutenant?'

'Damn it, bub, it doesn't matter! Sound Assembly.'

The brittle notes started from the brass mouth, and far downriver a white crane took wing in fright. The door of the house banged, and Byrne saw Davy skittering towards the corral, on hands and knees almost, the long rifle dragging. Five more minutes they waited, and then twelve men began to ford the river. They came casually, their horses picking the way with feet plunging and heads held up. The water splashed stains on the blue and white and yellow shirts of the riders, and beneath the hooves red mud whirled. When they reached the north bank they halted in line, facing the soldiers, and each man had a repeating rifle out of its scabbard and resting across the pommel.

Two rode up to Byrne and looked down at him with interest. The first man was tall, with a brown face that was tired, and creased by delicate lines, as if he had spent years savouring some distaste. He was chewing thoughtfully, and he spat carefully and politely downwind before he spoke.

'Name's Adams,' he said. 'Captain. Texas Rangers. Frontier Battalion.'

He wore a lion-skin vest, on which he rubbed the ball of his thumb as he waited. Byrne identified himself and his command.

The second man, sandy and freckled, and with surprisingly white hands, looked at the soldiers. 'God-damned niggers!' he said in loud disgust.

The captain tilted his chin towards the rise. 'You got Comanches over there. We killed one of them. You letting us through to the rest?'

'No sir,' said Byrne.

The Ranger leant both arms on his saddle-horn and stopped chewing. He looked at Byrne steadily, and his face seemed more weary than ever. 'Mister, I guess you don't understand. We've enough trouble with them on account of you bluecoats. You give them horses and rifles and let them out, and they come down on us in Texas.'

'These Indians have done no raiding.'

'Is that so?' said the captain, and he began to chew again.

'Damned nigger soldiers!' said the other man, as if he still could not believe what he saw.

'Captain Adams,' said Byrne, loudly, intending that this time the troopers should hear, 'that's the second time your friend has insulted the uniform and men of the United States Cavalry.'

'You hear that,' said the captain.

'I heard it,' said his lieutenant.

'Then don't insult the United States Cavalry.'

'No, Captain,' said the other man, and grinned.

'Now, lieutenant,' said Adams, 'tell those black boys to step aside and we'll go through.'

Byrne felt sweat itching on his brows, and it irked him to be on foot before these tall men. He wanted to look at the troopers to see how they were enduring this, but he knew that he could not. 'You're no longer in Texas,' he said, 'not once you've crossed that river. Those Comanches are under my protection.'

'Protection,' repeated the freckled man, and the word and the idea amused him.

The Ranger captain rubbed the ball of his thumb on his vest again, and he studied it closely. Then he returned his hands to the saddle-horn and stretched his body. 'Now, you should listen,' he said. 'Since Medicine Lodge Treaty, when you blue-coats started nursing them, the Comanches have killed fifty, maybe sixty people in Texas. Two weeks since they murdered a homesteader in Montagu County, a Mr Gottlieb Koozier it was. And they took Mrs Koozier and her kids over the river here.'

'Not these Comanche.'

'So you say,' said Adams patiently, 'but we figure it this way, what we get rid of now can't do no harm later.'

'They aren't wild animals.'

'Well now, you'd have to prove that to Mrs Koozier.'

'If you want a white woman's opinion of these Indians ask at the house down there.'

'We might do that,' said Adams, 'after we've caught them.'

'You have no legal right north of this river, sir.'

'That so?' said Adams, undisturbed. He nodded towards the Negro troopers. 'You aim to order them to fire on white folk, Mister?'

'If I am forced to,' said Byrne, and he unbuttoned his pistol holster.

'By God!' said the Ranger, 'I believe you would.' For a long time he stared at Byrne and then he spat, but this time it was not downwind. The yellow saliva spattered Byrne's boot.

'There's less'n ten of them,' said the sandy man.

'Shut up!' The Ranger captain pulled his horse about, digging his spurs into it. It went down the rise to the water in a sliding, skidding run. The sandy man looked at Byrne with his mouth slack. 'Nigger-lover!' he said, and before he turned his horse round he drove it forward, forcing Byrne to stumble back hurriedly.

The Rangers did not recross the water immediately. They waited, and Adams stood in the saddle, leaning his long body forward, jerking a finger towards the Indian camp. Two men walked their horses away from the column slowly, swinging ropes in their right hands, their heads bent at the neck. They looked up at the soldiers and they grinned. When they reached the scaffolding each man looped his rope lazily over the poles, turned the other end round his saddle-horn and rode into the river. The flimsy wood snapped and fell and kicked in the dust. Byrne saw the meat drifting away downstream. Then the Rangers, recoiling their ropes, walked out of the river and rode their horses backward and forward over the meat that had not been dragged into the water, churning it into the mud. The sport pleased them, and they began to yip, now spurring madly, pounding and pounding the Indian camp in the earth and the grass.

Byrne watched in hopeless despair, his hands behind his back, and the nails digging into the palms. The Comanches had come up from cover to the rim, silently, the wind moving among their feathers and fanning out the tails of their ponies. He knew that the Rangers were deliberately provoking them, and he wondered what he could do if, in their rage, the Comanches poured down through his thin skirmish line to attack the Texans. But they did not move. When the Rangers saw them one man shouted, and threw up his rifle, but Adams struck down the barrel, and even in his anger Byrne had to respect the captain, not for the humanity of the action but for the cunning of it. The Indians must fire first to place them and the soldiers in the wrong.

It was perhaps the overwhelming numbers of the Texans, and perhaps Quasia's uncertainty as to what Byrne might do, that prevented the Comanches from attacking. But as they watched the destruction of their camp they turned their ponies in despair, shook their weapons above their heads and cried out.

At last the twelve Texans rode back across the Red River to rejoin their main body, and then all of them moved in to the fold of high ground. The dust of their passing could be seen long after they had disappeared. A strange, sobbing sigh came from the Indians, and they began to move down the rise, in file with Quasia in the lead, his yellow pony putting its forefeet down stiffly. He did not look at Byrne as he rode by, but went

68

to the edge of the water and stared, with his hand across his eyes.

There was a figure lying limb-sprawled on the far bank. As Quasia kicked his horse forward Byrne shouted, and ran, waving his pistol. The Comanche looked with contempt at the stumbling officer and the flourishing gun, but he halted.

'Salem!' called Byrne, and he put the pistol away with embarrassment. 'See who it is,' he said, although he knew, as Quasia and all of them knew.

Salem brought the body over, its legs and arms stiff, and he put it down gently on the bank. It was Brown-Young-Man, and the Rangers had taken his scalp.

Byrne walked away. He stood with the water touching the soles of his boots and he looked across the river and swore. He swore in vicious, self-wounding blasphemy, the words coming from his lips on spittle.

'Sir?' It was Salem. His large, sensitive eyes were shadowed by the downward pull of his hat, his olive skin even more translucent in the growing dusk.

'What do you want?' said Byrne harshly. 'Another damned comment?'

'No sir. With the lieutenant's permission, I wished to thank him.'

'For what?'

'For the way he spoke up for his nigger soldiers.' Salem's lips twisted slightly, as if the words stung them.

Byrne looked at him in astonishment. 'You don't understand, do you?' he said. 'I don't give a damn for the colour of their skins. I don't love them because they're black, and I don't hate them either. I just don't care. But it was *my command* the man was talking about.'

'Yes sir,' said Salem, 'but they don't know it was that.'

Byrne pushed out his jaw. 'Salem, I don't care to discuss my motives and my actions with first sergeants, even though they may speak French and Spanish and have some knowledge of mathematics.'

'Yes, sir.'

'You don't like me much, do you, Salem? Why?'

69

'I hadn't thought about it, sir,' said the mulatto gently, and he saluted and went away.

There was never any delay between death and interment among the Comanche. Brown-Young-Man was buried that night in a deep wash upriver, where six pear-shaped rocks were lodged above the water. Directed by Whip-Owner, the chief mourner, the women prepared the body, washing it and sealing the eyes with red clay. They bound a blanket about it tightly and then they set it upon a horse. With the women riding on either side it was taken to the wash. There, in a hole dug beneath the stones, Brown-Young-Man was seated, his face to the east, and the stones were reassembled about him until he was hidden.

Whip-Owner shaved the hair from the left side of his head, a great sacrifice and testifying that Brown-Young-Man had been as close to him as a brother. He also cut the flesh of his arms and his chest and sang while the wounds bled. All the dead man's possessions were buried with him, all but his horse which Whip-Owner chose to keep as was his right. He cut the tail from it, and its mane, and when he had done this he went up on to the rise to sit by himself and to be lonely as custom demanded.

The other Indians built up their fire and walked about it singing. Their grieving went on for hour after hour, and Byrne sat with his shoulders against his saddle listening. There was no light in the house, and the woman had put shutters over the windows, and he knew that perhaps he should go down there to reassure her, but he had no wish for speech or company, even hers. The Indians' fire died down at last, from flames to glow, from glow to a spark lifting and spinning. Once he heard the sharp yelp of the dog and he sat forward quickly, his arms about his knees, and he remained thus for some time before he lay back and at last slept.

He was awakened by the sentry's anxious pull on his shoulder. It was not yet dawn but the moon had risen, and in its blue light he could see across to the other bank of the Red. The sentry was Cometoliberty, his face grey, and a shirt wrapped about his throat to keep out the cold. His eyes were wide and he could not speak, but he pointed down to the Indian camp.

There was nothing there. Indians, horses and mules had all gone. When Byrne went down he found the body of the dog lying beside the fire's ashes. It had been killed by an axe-blow on the skull so that it might not betray the Indians as they fled. Its body was stiff, and it had been dead for some time.

Colonel Benjamin Grierson's picket house was the only permanent building at Fort Sill that summer, excepting the sutler's store. He lived on the west bank of Medicine Bluff Creek, not far from the spot where General Sheridan's tent had been pitched during the winter campaign against the Cheyennes, and the white stone walk in front of his verandah had been laid there so that the general might not soil his boots when he walked to the mess tent. The rest of the post was a temporary affair, improvised by the troopers of the Tenth and the foot-soldiers of the Sixth Infantry who were Grierson's command in this area. They were camped in column of troops, each company being in line, and for the most part they lived in holes in the ground, made reasonably comfortable by brush roofs and sod fireplaces.

Smoke was drifting from the chimneys when Byrne stepped from the log slab hut which he shared with Harman, the other junior officer of Company M. The morning air was bright, and the sun glistened on the trampled mud of the company streets. Along the picket-lines black troopers were answering morning work call, clanking buckets, calling, shouting. Byrne could hear the sound of distant axes to the north where the quartermaster's teams were cutting down a stand of oak to build a more permanent post. The whole green valley was full of noise, the creak of waggon wheels, the mournful obscenities of the teamsters, the singing orders of a sergeant who was patiently drilling a platoon of the Sixth on a flat meadow by the creek.

In a grove beyond this meadow were the lodges of a Kiowa village, newly come to take the white man's road and the white man's annuity until the old passions seduced them again.

Byrne's pleasure in the morning was reluctant, for he was experiencing a discomfort that was both mental and physical. He was wearing, for the first time, his shell-jacket, and it was tight beneath the arms. The dark blue chasseur cap, with its too-shiny peak, gripped his forehead, and he wished that he had at least had time to get his hair cut. It was a mistake, he knew now, for him to have buckled on his dress belt, the four stripes of gold lace and the interweaving of yellow silk. Had Harman been on the post, and not away on detail escorting one of Grierson's hardware trains from Arbuckle, Byrne would have asked his advice, for Harman was no sergeant turned officer but had been a volunteer captain during the war and knew what an officer should and should not wear when called before his colonel on reprimand.

Grierson was using his house as post headquarters until the quartermaster's men built something more convenient. There was a fine black horse outside, its furniture made of blue velvet instead of felt, and edged with yellow silk instead of flannel. The bridle was held by a mulatto orderly whose uniform had obviously passed through the improving hands of the post tailor, for it fitted his superb body like a skin. The tilt of his cap, strapped below his chin, was as rakish as that of a general's aide. He saluted Byrne, and stared at him with an expression in which curiosity, sympathy and amusement were all mixed, thus informing Byrne that the whole post knew why Grierson had called for him.

But the sight of the Colonel's horse restored some of the lieutenant's self-respect. Its presence there, before the commander's quarters, was an innocent irony. Everybody knew that Grierson, one of the war's most successful cavalrymen, and the leader of the great raid from Tennessee to Baton Rouge, disliked horses and rode when necessary only.

The outer room of the house, when Byrne stepped into it from the ramada, was full of junior officers from the companies. Few of the Arkansas plantation hands who had become troopers of the Tenth could read or write, and the clerical duties, usually performed by second-enlistment corporals and sergeants, had to be carried out by lieutenants. They sat, capless and with arms bent, at tables, working on the letters, reports and inventories which gave joy to Grierson's orderly mind.

Alvord, commander of Company M and the post's adjutant, looked up as Byrne entered. He was a wearied, conscientious man, a career soldier who, without his being able to do much about it, found himself ensnared by paper work. He was older than Byrne, short and greying, his mind always perplexed by a second problem while he discussed the first. He nodded to Byrne, his hands scuffling across the desk until they grasped and lifted two yellow sheets of paper which Byrne recognized as his own report of the patrol. Alvord read them through slowly, pulling at his lower lip with finger and thumb. Then he gestured vaguely towards a chair and went into the next room.

Byrne stood where he was, his head up, his cap tucked into the crook of his arm, and his eyes staring at the wall. He was standing, he knew, as an enlisted man might stand when called to the regimental office. Any of the young men now whispering at their desks behind him would have relaxed had they been in his position, even joked about it. Byrne wondered if the fact that he could see no humour in the situation was a fault or a virtue. He did not think it mattered.

When Alvord opened the inner door and stood aside, Byrne walked straight in and clicked his heels, cursing inwardly because the noise was too loud. It was a sparsely furnished room, a chair, a field-desk, an iron-bound trunk and a canvas basin. Against the wall was a camp-bed on which lay Grierson's violin.

The bow was in the Colonel's fine white hands, and he was sitting on one corner of his desk with a leg swinging. He was a tall man with mild, friendly eyes and a great beak of a nose. His hair grew thick on the crown of his head like a roach, and his brown beard had been fluffed into a bush about his gentle mouth. He wore a single-breasted sack-coat sashed with red. On the desk in front of him was a plain, black felt hat with no badge.

He passed a ball of rosin up the hairs of the bow. 'Sit down, lieutenant, if you wish.'

'Thank you, sir,' said Byrne, but he remained standing.

Grierson looked at the bow. 'I've not seen you at our musical evenings?'

'No sir. I don't believe you've held one since I joined.'

Grierson laughed. 'Sir, will you sit down? You're not a non-com on report.' It was meant well, Byrne knew, but the underlying reminder of what he had once been, and of the brevity of his commissioned service, did not make him feel at ease. Perhaps Grierson saw this, for he brought the chair from behind the desk, putting his hand on the lieutenant's shoulder and pressing him into it. Then he sprawled on the bed, crossing his legs and tapping the bow on the palm of his left hand. He realized that this stiff-necked man was going to be difficult and he sighed softly.

'My compliments on your report, Mister,' he said. 'It was most informative.'

'Thank you, sir.'

'You seem to have handled the situation commendably, up to a point. You understand what I mean?'

'Yes, sir.'

'You failed to put a sentry on the Comanche camp after that business with the Rangers, and they foxed you.'

'Yes, sir.'

Grierson sat up, put the bow on the blanket beside him, and rested his hands on his knees. He stared at Byrne's broken profile, and he wished the man would make the interview easier by looking at him.

'You had the damnedest luck, Mr Byrne. Those Indians might easily have gone over the river into Texas instead of coming back here.'

'Yes, sir, I am aware of that.'

'I got a complaint this morning from the Rangers. They say the Comanches had been raiding over on their side.'

'Not Quasia's band, sir. Veal followed their trail. It came straight back to the agency. In my view, sir ... Have I permission to express it?'

'Oh, yes,' said Grierson resignedly, 'by all means.' He flicked the fingers of his right hand upward through his beard.

'Quasia returned to tell Brown-Young-Man's relatives so that they might go into mourning.'

'He could have come back just as easily under escort.'

Byrne flushed. 'Yes, sir. I'm making no excuses.'

'I should hope not,' said Grierson jovially. He plucked a string of the violin, and then another, frowned, and turned a key.

'If the Colonel will permit . . .'

'Of course, forgive me,' Grierson put down the violin.

'Quasia did not regard my command as a guard, sir. He figured we were there to protect him. When we failed . . .' His voice hesitated over the word. 'When that didn't happen he took his own steps. In my opinion, sir, the murder was a serious provocation.'

'Are you pleading for him, lieutenant?'

'No, sir. Those are the facts as I see them.'

'And as you've already put them in your report.' Grierson grasped a knee in both hands and rocked his body slowly. 'But you don't say why the two Indians were allowed to get across the Red.'

'No sir. I accept responsibility for that mistake.'

'No real harm has been done, you know, Mister,' said Grierson, in another effort to put the lieutenant at ease, but Byrne, unable to see how the death of Brown-Young-Man could be so casually dismissed, made no comment.

'A week ago,' said Grierson conversationally, 'the Texans sent me the heads of three Comanches pickled in jars of alcohol. They believed the men could be identified as agency Indians whom we had allowed to cross into Texas on raids. As it turned out we had never seen them before, but the incident does give us an idea of how delicate the situation is, don't you think?'

'Yes, sir.'

'Yes,' said Grierson. He got up from the bed and stood by the desk, parting the papers on it with a forefinger. 'I believe, lieutenant, that you were unsuccessful in obtaining a commission in a white regiment?'

'Yes, sir.'

'Wouldn't you care to relax a little?'

'Thank you, sir,' said Byrne, but he scarcely moved.

'Would I be correct', asked Grierson, combing his beard again, 'in assuming that you therefore regard service in a coloured regiment as second-best?'

'I hadn't thought of it that way, sir.'

'It would be a logical conclusion, wouldn't it? Wouldn't the argument go something like this – you are not considered good enough for a white regiment but you are given a commission with the Tenth? *Ergo*, coloured regiments are inferior to white.'

'I have not so argued,' said Byrne hoarsely.

'I don't believe you, Mister.'

'With the Colonel's permission, is this relevant?'

'Your reluctance to discuss it makes it so, Mr Byrne.'

'Yes, sir.' Byrne looked at the wall, and then said, 'I'm aware that many white officers are unwilling to serve in coloured regiments, and officers must be found.'

'From second-best material like yourself? Is that what you think?'

Byrne did not reply, and Grierson's voice was no longer gentle. 'I asked you a direct question, Mister!'

'It's not a fair question, sir.'

'Maybe not,' sighed Grierson, 'but I think you've answered it for me.' He went back to the bed, and Byrne, his eyes still fixed on the wall, could hear the dry squeal of the rosin passing up and down the bow. 'I'd like to put you straight on a little recent history, Mr Byrne. Since this regiment was formed three years ago it has seen more field service than any white cavalry regiment in the west. It has been in action against the Cheyenne on the Kansas frontier. It was engaged in the winter campaign against Black Kettle. Units of it rescued Major Forsyth's command on the Arickaree. Captain Carpenter's company served with distinction in the Beaver Creek fight. Do you know all this, Mr Byrne?'

'Yes, sir, I do.'

'Are you proud of it?' He did not wait for a reply. 'Calico Troop mainly consists of recruits, Mr Byrne?'

'Yes, sir.'

'What's your opinion of Negroes, Mister?'

'I have none, sir.'

'That's a damn-fool answer!'

'If you say so, sir.'

'I do, so think of a better one.'

'I find it difficult to express an opinion on the subject.'

'Then I'll ask another question,' said Grierson, his patient tone too emphatic to be sincere. 'What's your opinion of the Comanches?'

'Do you mean the policy of the Indian Office, sir?'

'No, damn it, I don't! I mean would you pickle their heads in alcohol?'

'No sir, the Comanches are human beings.'

'Just a little bit more human than Negroes, eh, Mister?'

Byrne was now too weary to be angry, and he had the insane impulse to say that he would be happier if all Negroes, all Comanches and all colonels were submerged in the ocean. He wondered if Grierson put all his officers through this harsh catechism on human rights. He said, 'I try to do my duty without considering the colour of a man's skin, sir.'

'That's a pious bit of self-deception, Mr Byrne. In this regiment it is important for you to remember that you *are* dealing with men of colour, red and black, and that to them the most important thing about you is that you are *white*. You are saddled with the problem and its responsibilities, Mister, whether you like it or not.'

'Yes, sir.'

'Yes,' said Grierson. 'And remember that whoever else gets the glory for the pacification of the West, the Afro-American troopers of the Tenth will probably have done most of the hard work.' He arose from the bed and stood in front of Byrne, forcing the lieutenant to look at him. He smiled pleasantly, his red cheeks appling on either side of his great nose. 'Now how did we get to quarrelling about all this? You'll have to forgive me, lieutenant.'

'The Colonel has been very instructive,' said Byrne cautiously.

'Has he now?' Grierson laughed. 'Sometimes I forget that I'm no longer a school teacher in Illinois. This Comanche of yours, what's his name, Quasia? What's he like?'

'A young man, sir. Proud and brave. He has a chip on his shoulder, of course, like all young Indians. But he can be trusted implicitly so long as he is not betrayed.'

'And he has been betrayed?'

'I believe he may think so, sir. The killing of Brown-Young-Man, I mean, and the hide-hunters being south of the Arkansas instead of north where the Comanches were told they would be kept.'

'Do you think he may be inclined to lead a vengeance raid into Texas?'

'I think it's possible, sir.'

'Well, then,' said Grierson cheerfully, 'we'll have to make sure that he doesn't, won't we? Mr Tatum tells me that the Indians under his care are responding well and have manifested a desire to have their lands broken and fenced...'

'The Caddoes and Wichitas, yes, sir.'

'Don't interrupt me, Mr Byrne. Mr Tatum says that *all* the Indians realize that they must now grow their own food, now that the buffalo is disappearing. That is Mr Tatum's view, and I agree with it.' He looked at the expression on Byrne's face, and he added sharply, 'And I don't give a damn for any contrary opinion you may hold, Mr Byrne.'

'With the Colonel's permission, I don't think the change can come this quickly.'

'Why not?'

'Perhaps because most of the Comanches, the Kwahadis particularly, are not on the reservation at all,' said Byrne, sourly relishing the point of debate.

'This is a big country, Mr Byrne, but it's getting smaller every year. Settlers are not going to wait until we have talked the Indians on to reservations, nor are the ranchers and the railroads. Irreconcilables like your Quasia are a bad example to the hostiles, and can't be allowed to run around loose. We deal with them firmly and the others will soon come to heel. Mr Tatum is bringing him up here this afternoon, and he'll be arrested and held pending a decision from the Department. All right, Mr Byrne, that's all!'

As Byrne stepped out on to the ramada he heard the first notes of *O, Susannah!* leaping sprightly from the strings of the colonel's violin.

When the lieutenant returned to Grierson's house that afternoon he saw that a detachment of twelve men from Company A was drawn up in line before the white stone walk, with an officer and trumpeter, and the company guidon snapping. They sat erect, chasseur caps pulled down and shading their eyes, beads of sweat shining on their dark cheeks and rolling down to stain their bandannas. They had sabres drawn, and Byrne thought that this was as melodramatic as it was probably unnecessary. The light breeze, too hot to cool the air, whipped the dust into caracoles about the fetlocks of the bay horses.

Grierson was sitting on a wicker chair beneath the shade of the ramada roof, fanning himself with a sheaf of papers. With him, and standing, were Alvord, Lieutenant-Colonel Davidson, and Majors Forsyth and Kidd of the Tenth. For some reason that Byrne could not imagine, Chaplain Grimes and two civilian contractors were also there. When he reported, the Colonel greeted him amiably, and suggested that he wait on the verandah, too, out of the sun. He stood with his back against the wall of the house, and when he looked through the window he saw that the room beyond was full of infantrymen, armed and with bayonets fixed.

As time passed Grierson grew restless, consulting his watch several times and staring down the valley. At half-past four a party of Indians came up from the south, more than a hundred of them, men and women, unarmed and mostly on foot. At their head was Tatum, and with him were four of his Quaker employees from the agency.

When they reached the house the Indians grouped themselves into a half moon, the right horn of which stretched over the creek into the oak grove on the other side. Those who were horsed were the agency chiefs, led by Mow-way, the only Kwahadi leader on the reservation, and even he was not a true Kwahadi, but a Kotchateka who had touched the pen at the Medicine Lodge Council and brought his people into the reservation, recognizing not the justice of the treaty but the fact that the white men were too many to fight for ever.

A chair was brought for him, and he sat on it in the sun facing the ramada. He was a middle-aged, impressive man with fine features, his eyes blood-shot and short-sighted. His scalp-lock was held by the claw of a bear that he had killed in his youth, and he wore a white man's black vest over his white shirt. His broad mouth reflected his friendly nature, and he sat at ease, brushing the flies from his face. His leggings were of fine blue cloth, piped with yellow, and now and then, unconsciously almost, he passed a fat hand along them admiringly. Next to him was another Comanche, Horseback, a tall Yapparika chief with a black and thoughtless face. And beside him was Lone Wolf, a Kiowa, whose eyes moved suspiciously across the faces of the white men. He pointed to the mounted troopers and spoke sharply, but Mow-Way smiled and shook his head. Byrne realized that none of them knew why they had been brought here.

Some of the Indians were dressed in the cheap clothing that had been given them the previous December on Annuity Day, hard hats and black coats of serge. There were women wearing white cotton stockings, and some of the men wore such stockings on the arms, with the feet cut off. Byrne looked at them until he found Quasia. The young man was standing with his arms folded on his chest, a single feather in his scalp-lock, and his smooth face empty. With him were Red-Buffalo and Whip-Owner. The sun fell on the brass gorget at Red-Buffalo's throat and on the mallard's feathers in his braided hair. Whip-Owner's head was still shaved on the left side, and the scabs of the ritual cuts were black on his breast and arms. When Quasia saw Byrne on the ramada there was no recognition in his face.

Tatum and his colleagues sat on a bench opposite the Indian leaders, so that they, the troopers and the chiefs made three sides of a square before the house. The light was harsh and green on the Quakers' dark clothes.

Grierson began the talk by greeting Mow-Way amiably. Matthew Leeper, the agency interpreter, stood in front of the ramada, between officers and the Indians, turning his body this way and that to translate. Grierson said that he had been very disturbed by reports from Texas that young Kiowas and Comanches from the reservation were raiding across the Red River again. He rose from the wicker chair and moved to the edge of the verandah, the sun falling on his face and glinting in his brown beard. He hammered home his words by beating a fist into the palm of his hand. He mocked anger so theatrically that Byrne wondered if it could possibly delude the Indians. They watched the Colonel's performance impassively and without comment.

When Leeper finally asked Mow-Way to speak the old man began by pointing to the troopers. Why, he asked, were the buffalo soldiers there with knives in their hands? The People had been asked to come to this talk without arms, and they had done so. But the pony soldiers had weapons and this made him unhappy and afraid.

Grierson smiled. Was Mow-Way certain that none of his young men had guns concealed beneath their blankets? This was either tactless, or deliberately provocative, and Byrne, watching the anger in Mow-Way's face, could not understand Grierson's intention. Although it was probable that some of the young Indians, in the mutual distrust that characterized such talks as this, had brought arms with them, it scarcely seemed wise to make an issue out of it.

With his hands, and in the slow, musical voice, Mow-Way explained that he did not understand Grierson's anger. It was true that some Texans had been killed, but it was equally true that a number of Indians had been killed also. He had taken the white man's road to stop this senseless business. If Grierson would tell him who, among the Comanches, had broken the law his policemen would punish them.

Grierson considered this for a moment and then, with another patently false demonstration of anger, he said that he had heard often enough from the Comanches and Kiowas themselves that they were men of honour, but although they had

82

accepted the white man's gifts they had not given up their bad ways. This was the behaviour of coyotes.

This appeared to be a second tactical mistake. When Leeper translated the words the Kiowa, Lone Wolf, stood up and drew his blanket about his hips. He raised his fist and shouted at the ramada. Then he stalked away, with the rest of the Kiowas following him. There was a movement among the Comanches, too, but Mow-Way held up his hand, and called, and stopped it. He looked at the Colonel. He thought, he said, that Grierson had some other motive for calling The People here than talking to them as if they were disobedient children.

Grierson, who had watched the departure of the Kiowas with evident satisfaction, nodded his head. He had indeed something important to say. He wanted to talk to the young man called Eagle-Tail-Feather. Now it was Mow-Way's turn to play-act, and he put an expression of great surprise on his face. Why should the Colonel be interested in so insignificant a young man? Fanning himself with a lazy hand he was prepared to discuss the point when Quasia resolved the argument by stepping forward. He folded his arms and looked boldly at the blue and yellow grouping of the officers on the ramada, loudly asking what was wanted of him. Surprisingly, Grierson asked him if he felt any fear.

The Indian frowned at the unexpected question. He put his hand on his chest above the heart. He said that Grierson, if he stepped down and placed a hand there too, would feel no scare.

Grierson smiled. He had not meant to insult Quasia, but he believed that a young man who had behaved so badly, and brought such disgrace to his people, must surely feel shame if not fear. Quasia was puzzled. He turned his head over his shoulder to Mow-Way and then he looked back at the officers.

At that moment there was a cry from the side of the house. Some of the Indian women, bored with the council, had walked away from it earlier to inspect the soldiers' camp. Two of them had looked through the window of Grierson's house and seen the soldiers there. Now they called an alarm, and there was sudden confusion. The seated Indians jumped to their feet, while others surged towards the house. More began to run down the hill in fear. Somewhere a bugle brayed, and the post-guard came running, rifles held against their chests, their bayonets shining. On the ramada Grierson shouted, his hand outstretched, and the infantrymen poured from the door behind him. A horse began to squeal.

Quasia stood in the dust with his feet apart, his arms loose and his head swinging from side to side in desperation. The mounted men and the foot-soldiers closed about him, pricking him in the back with sabres and bayonets, and urging him towards the guard-house. Agent Tatum stood below the porch, his hat off, his bald head gleaming, and his voice shouting an incoherent protest.

The Comanches swayed backward and forward dangerously, and because he saw no weapons in their hands Byrne realized, with surprise, that after all they had honoured the conditions of the council. Even so they threatened to throw themselves on the bayonets, and the lieutenant in charge of the foot-soldiers ran forward with a blanket which he threw over Quasia's head so that the young man might not see and might not take advantage of any attempt to rescue him. Then, his face red and his mouth open, the lieutenant shouted to his men to take their prisoner to the guard-house as quickly as possible.

Byrne watched with ineffectual disapproval. He was deafened by the noise, and jostled by the excited officers who crowded forward to the rail. One of the civilian contractors took a small derringer pistol from his pocket and waved it dramatically at the mob of Indians. He yelled like a man at a horse-race.

Quasia tripped and stumbled down the gentle hill, hands thrust blindly from beneath the blanket. About him and behind him were the foot-soldiers with their prodding bayonets, and behind them was the skirmish line of troopers, sabres slanting and sweating faces turned back towards the following Comanches. The Indians shouted hoarsely, calling for Mow-Way, but the old man was lost somewhere in the dust.

Byrne pushed his way to the end of the ramada, anxious only to get away from the maddened excitement, but once there his eye was caught by a flash of colour above the backs

84

of the mules in the corral. He saw the waving of an Indian blanket, and then an Indian himself, fat Kills-Something sitting astride a mule yelling. Even as Byrne shouted a warning to Grierson the rails of the corral went down, and a flood of frightened animals poured over them, urged on now by Red-Buffalo and Whip-Owner.

The herd swerved in a wave by the back of the Colonel's house, plunged through his vegetable garden and down the hill. The line of troopers and infantrymen paused for a moment and then scattered. Quasia, the blanket dragged from his head, waited for the mules, and when they enveloped him in dust, rocking heads and kicking heels, he swung himself easily to the back of one of them. His friends gobbled in high triumph, and they drove on the stampede towards the high ground of Medicine Bluff.

A bugler, standing below the ramada, blew his excited calls, but the efforts of the soldiers to assemble were hampered by the rest of the Indians who, in real or assumed panic, ran aimlessly about the post area, fluttering their arms and hooting like owls, frightening the horses into rearing disorder. It was twenty minutes before a squadron rode out at the gallop.

It returned to the post at sunset. The mules had been scattered between the horn of Medicine Bluffs and the grove of oaks two miles to the east at Heyl's Hole. There was no sign of Quasia and the other Indians. At any point of the run they could have slipped away, screened by the high ground. Grierson took two companies down to the agency buildings within the hour. Tatum, alarmed and unhappy, stood in his shirt-sleeves before his house and would answer no questions until he had made a formal protest. Grierson listened to it impatiently, and when it was finished said, sarcastically, that of course the agent had been unaware of his intention to arrest Quasia.

'It was not thy intention, sir, but the method . . .'

'Mr Tatum, you may try to pray an Indian into my guard-house any day you like. Until you succeed I'll do it my way. Have you any news of these young men?'

Tatum knew nothing. A party of Comanches had ridden to

his house not long before the Colonel's arrival, and had accused him of being responsible for the attempt to arrest Quasia. They seemed to be drunk (and he would like to make a formal protest against the illegal sale of spirits to the Indians). They had flourished weapons and declared themselves ready to cut out his heart. He did not think the Comanches were likely to tell him anything now.

But the next morning Mow-Way, mounted on a white horse and wearing his war-bonnet, came to Grierson's house accompanied by a council of old men. Without expressing either approval or disapproval by his face or words, he said that he wished the Colonel to know that Eagle-Tail-Feather, Red-Buffalo, War-Axe, Whip-Owner, Kills-Something, Woman's-Heart and Broken-Neck had left the reservation. They had taken spare horses.

Grierson combed his fingers through his beard nervously. He demanded that Mow-Way send his policemen to bring the boys back, but the old man refused politely. He spoke earnestly to the interpreter Leeper, repeating the words again and again. The warriors, he said, were all *tuivitsi*, all young and unmarried men and headstrong. Even had he wished, he could not have stopped them. On occasions like this, when they had been betrayed by the white men, they were inclined to remember that their accepted leader was Quanah Parker who still lived outside the reservation on the Staked Plains.

When Grierson asked if Mow-Way believed that the young men intended to raid into Texas in revenge for the killing of Brown-Young-Man, the old man nodded sadly. Then he made the sign for no more talk and rode away.

Grierson turned about, so that no Indian looking back in curiosity might see the anger in his face. He stood erect, his mild eyes unusually hot as he looked at Byrne.

'Well, Mister? You see? You'll take that miserable patrol of yours out at dawn, and you'll bring me back that Indian before he does any damage!' He did not wait for Byrne's salute, nor acknowledge it when he heard the lieutenant's hand flap to his cap. He walked stiff-legged and straight-backed to his house.

Byrne sat in his hut. The hurricane lamp was on the floor

and the calcimined walls sweated in the heat of it. There was mist on his spectacles, too, and he rubbed them impatiently with the ball of his thumb, looping them over his ears again. He stared at the pad of paper on his knee and he pushed his tongue into his cheek. He felt for the jug of corn-whiskey without looking, picked it up and drank from the neck. He had drunk a lot already, but it had had no effect on him beyond making him sweat. He pulled his blouse loose across his chest and tried to write again.

The trouble was, he was not sure what it was he wished to say. He rested the pencil on the paper.

Colonel B. H. Grierson, U.S.C.,
Commanding Post,
Fort Sill, Ind. Terr.

Sir: As a result of the damnable mockery of your attempt to arrest the Comanche Eagle-Tail-Feather for no evident crime beyond his natural reaction to the death of a friend, I feel compelled ...

No, that wasn't it either. It had nothing to do with Quasia or Grierson's conduct, not immediately. His feelings were far more subjective. He screwed up the paper and felt for the jug, and when he had drunk from it and stared aggressively at the wall for some time, he wrote again.

Sir: Yesterday you implied that I did not believe that negroes were capable of satisfactory service in the United States Cavalry. You also implied that I considered myself (in your own words) second-best choice as officer material.

You are, as commander of this post, entitled to unequivocal answers to both of these suggestions. Whatever their incidental achievements as infantrymen during the late war (for which their natural desire for liberty may have been in part responsible) I do not believe that Africans can make cavalrymen in peacetime, lacking the spirit, endurance and extreme courage demanded by this arm in the Department of Missouri.

This view, I believe, is shared by many white officers who are naturally reluctant therefore to assume command in a negro regiment. The Army is thus forced to find officers where it can, and among men to whom it would not normally give command. I have no doubt that this is why I was chosen.

You further questioned me on my attitude toward men of colour. I do not believe an officer or non-commissioned officer should concern himself with such matters. He should not be involved personally in controversies that injure the service. It is regrettable that they should be forced upon an officer in a command like this.

I am aware that I should have given all this more serious consideration before ...

He stopped and read what he had written, and when he had read it again he shook his head slowly and smiled. He sat with his hands resting on the paper and his eyes staring through his spectacles at the blurred wall opposite, until he finally lifted the hurricane lamp and held the letter in its flame. He watched the paper burn, dropping the last fragment to the floor.

The jug was empty, and he yawned and turned to his blankets.

They left early in the morning, when the rearguard of night still held the oak groves. They were not entirely the patrol that had ridden on the buffalo hunt. The scout was now an old and full-blooded Wichita whose name, Nasthoe, appeared on the muster-roll in its English translation, Shot-in-the-foot. Christian Veal, sick with a fever, had been replaced by a boy called Cato Brown, a slim and melancholy recruit with frightened eyes. He was a poor horseman, and this destroyed any sympathy Byrne might have felt when he saw the rosary beneath the trooper's bandanna. Each man carried one hundred rounds of carbine ammunition and thirty-six of pistol. Their cantle-rolls contained forty-eight pounds of oats, enough for six days if stretched. In the *aparejos*, strapped to the two pack-mules, was forage for three more days, as well as hardtack, sugar, coffee and a supply of salt. The troopers wore fatigue uniforms, shirts, suspenders and felt hats. They had ponchos held by coat-straps below the pommel, carbines booted on the right side.

They rode out at dawn when reveille was sounding, and before smoke had begun to rise from the sod chimneys of the dug-outs. It was cold, and the troopers bit on their chin leathers to stop their chattering teeth. Byrne, his head heavy and his mouth sour from the night's jug, had said nothing to them when he inspected them in the misted blue light of the parade, nothing beyond the old first-sergeant's exhortation *'Ride the horse all the way!'* For half an hour they did not speak either, and then the lifting sun, rolling brown over the land, thawed their voices. Above the noise of steel and leather Byrne heard Attucks' bass mocking Honesty.

'You know we going to the great American desert, man?'

'That so?'

'That so. Man, they got serpents there so ornery they can kill you with a spit. Ain't that so, Uncle?'

Nathan Donethegetaway's gentle voice was noncommittal. 'I heard tell, Corporal.'

'You hear, Honesty man? Uncle says so. Them snakes'll make short work of you, Honesty.'

'Ain't no such snakes.'

'You know for sure, man?'

'I ain't saying that.'

'If'n you don't know for certain sure, how come you say there ain't such snakes?'

'You fooling me, Jonathan?'

'Man, I couldn't fool nobody with a name like Honesty.'

They rode to the west and south, with flankers out at right and left point, eight hundred yards ahead. They marched at the walk for two miles, and then for a mile at the trot. For ten minutes in the hour they dismounted and walked by the bridle. They nooned below a bluff which stood like a cliff against the westward ocean of the plains, and Byrne's order to fill canteens from a creek was the first word he had spoken since leaving the post. They rode on, and now the sun was in their faces, pulling down the heads of the horses, and flies clung to the sweat on their flanks. Yet, and Byrne wondered strangely at this, Miles James sang in a sweet tenor, as if he had a wall against his back and all day to do nothing but laze. Attucks now mocked Riddle.

'Riddle, you hear that boy singing? You figure we need a music-man like you with us?'

Riddle did not reply.

'Riddle, you play that bugle in the war?'

Still the trumpeter did not reply.

'Riddle, man, you're a mighty talkative nigger.'

At three in the afternoon Byrne halted the patrol, and then bivouacked in a shallow wash with three sentries out, one on the horse-line and one at either end of the wash. When he had eaten, Nasthoe came to Byrne, picking his few teeth with one hand, and pulling the bridle of his ewe-necked horse with the other. He would go on a scout, he said. He was almost bald, which was rare in an Indian. His grey hair hung in uneven strands from the tonsure at the centre of his skull, and he pushed them from his eyes when he put on his hat. He wore a blue jacket and dirty buckskin leggings, and he carried an old Springfield carbine, from the muzzle of which hung two turkey's feathers. There was a turkey feather in his hat, too. He was extraordinarily ugly, but his eyes were shrewd.

He returned an hour after dusk as tirelessly as he had ridden out. He had seen no Comanche sign, but he had seen the trail of a great buffalo herd, and in the far distance, against the set of the sun, he had seen buzzards dropping from the sky, indicating that somebody had made a surround. He did not think the hunters had been Indians. He had heard, though faintly, the sound of buffalo rifles.

The patrol moved at dawn, and an hour later Byrne halted to tighten girths and to allow the horses to drink from their riders' hats. He inspected the pack-mules and found that a canvas cincha, rotted by urine, had broken through half of its width. He swore at Salem, but he knew that if anybody were to blame it was himself. An hour and a half were wasted while a new cincha was improvised from one of the double-sacks of the rations. He told the packers to keep an eye on the cincha, but just after two o'clock it broke again, and Byrne ordered a halt for the day.

They were only thirty-five miles from the post, and they should have been fifty. He entered the time, the distance, and the cause of the delay in his notebook, without comment. His thoughts dwelt ironically on the belief that a cavalry patrol, hampered by pack-mules, and limited to twenty-five miles a day, could pursue, overtake and engage a party of Indians who were able to ride eighty miles in twenty-four hours without tiring themselves or their ponies. Quasia, he was sure, had by now joined Quanah Parker on the Staked Plains, or ridden far south into Texas. He put the notebook away with his spectacles and stared across to the two troopers who, under Salem's direction, were repairing the cincha. One of them was James, and of course the boy was singing.

> 'O, you read in the Bible and you understand
> Methuselah was a witness for my Lord.
> O, who'll be a witness?
> Who'll be a witness for my Lord?'

Nasthoe came in before dusk, and rode up to Byrne without dismounting. He pointed to the west. 'White man,' he said. 'Hour. Maybe dead now.'

Byrne called up Attucks and Honesty and left at the gallop with Nasthoe. They first saw the white man when he was a mile away, a solitary figure on the rippling grass. He was moving curiously, first running, then walking and sometimes crawling on all fours. Byrne fired his pistol, and although the man must have heard it there was no response from him. When they neared him, and above the rush of the wind, Byrne heard the croaking, grating obscenities coming from the man's throat. He blundered into them blindly, his arms outstretched, and when he lurched against Nasthoe's horse the Wichita put out a foot and casually pushed him away. He fell on his back and lay there, with his mouth open and his voice rasping into silence.

'*Damn you heathen!*' said Byrne to Nasthoe, and he dismounted. 'Canteen!' he called, and felt Honesty thrust one into his hand. He wet the neckerchief and wiped the cloth across the black lips. The man was a buffalo hunter, a skinner by the stench of him, his hide jacket stained by old blood and caked with grease. He died with his head on Byrne's knee, his eyes slipping slowly upward until they were two yellow marbles in his black and bearded face. When Byrne lowered the body to the earth his hand discovered the broken haft of an arrow in the man's back.

Nasthoe touched the wood curiously. Then he grasped it and pulled with surprising strength. The barb came out with a wrench of flesh. The Wichita wiped it with a handful of grass, and then held it before Byrne, pointing to the two black grooves on one side of the haft, and the red spiral groove on the other. 'Comanche,' he said.

There was nothing in the man's pockets to identify him – a bag of tobacco which Nasthoe put in his shirt, a piece of paper obviously from a theatre bill and showing a girl kicking a leg high from her skirts, and, inexplicably, two bright pieces of mica which may once have pleased his childish mind and been saved by him as a talisman.

There was nowhere to bury him that would be safe from the coyotes, no stones to cover him, and they left him there on his back, with his mouth open and his eyes turned inward.

They found the hide-hunters' camp the next day, cutting the waggon-trail and following it. The camp was in a wide draw, and the hunters had obviously been there for some time. There were three big waggons, all loaded with skins, and some attempt had been made to burn them. The front wheels of one had collapsed, spilling the waggon over so that the hides had flaked out like the leaves of a book. They were charred and curled at the edges.

The troopers rode in and looked down at the bodies of five men, staring in immobilized fascination until Byrne shouted at them, and rode against them with his horse, his face scarlet.

The camp had been surprised, for there were no empty shells on the earth to show that there had been a fight. The dead men were tied at the wrists and feet with rawhide, and two were still bound to the wheels of a waggon. They were naked, and each had been cut many times with knives on the chest and arms. Three were tongueless, and all of them had been emasculated. A final hatchet blow on the skull had mercifully killed them.

Nasthoe looked at the dead men and shrugged his shoulders. He walked about their camp, touching the earth with his fingers, picking up a broken stem of grass and holding it before his face, walking out a way to the west or the south and then returning to stare at the way he had walked. When he had done all this several times he came to Byrne with a smirk of pride. He said, 'Comanche.'

The idiocy of the obvious information irritated Byrne, but he kept his temper. 'How many?' he said.

'Five. Maybe, six, seven. Take three of white men's horses. Ride there. Maybe there.'

'But which way, Nasthoe?'

The Wichita spread out his hands. That would take a longer scout, he said. He had great respect for the Comanches' cunning. Byrne sent him to find out, and when he had told Attucks to organize a burial party he turned his back on the camp. He was surprised by the terrible weakness in the pit of his back.

There were many false trails, but in the end Nasthoe found the true one. It led towards the Red River. When the Comanches' night-camp was found, on the southern side of a rise, there were signs at the top of the hill that they had kept a watch to the north and thus expected pursuit. At the river, to Byrne's uneasy surprise, the trail turned westward towards Norvall's Crossing. The march was hard across the saline flats, through spreads of wiry grass, and then, approximately five miles from the crossing, the trail led into the river. Byrne sent Salem and two troopers across to the other bank, but they found no spot where the Indians might have emerged. It was unlikely, he thought, that the Comanches would have gone eastward towards the crowded cattle trails. Their logical objective must be either the Staked Plains or the old Kiowa and Comanche war road through Texas to the Rio Grande.

With the trail lost there was nothing he could do but push on towards the crossing, and there to halt for a day perhaps while Nasthoe went out on an extended scout. This decision pleased him for reasons beyond its tactical value. He was anxious to see Anne Norvall again.

He knew, by the direction of its approach, that the patrol would be seen from the way-house when it was still two miles away on the high bluffs. So that the woman might not be alarmed, he halted there and ordered Riddle to sound a call. The clear challenge hung on the air, and he took his glass and focused it on the house. He saw the light splash of the woman's apron across the open door, the tiny figures of Davy and Jinny, and when he turned the glass towards the corral he saw that there was another horse there beside the old grey. A man was there too, a white man, his elbows resting on the rail and his face turned towards the sound of the bugle. *'Damn!'* said Byrne to himself softly, without knowing why the presence of the man irritated him.

Within the half-hour the patrol was dismounting by the cottonwoods where Quasia had made camp the week before. Anne Norvall ran from the house towards him, her skirts lifted by both hands, and her body swaying as women's bodies move when they run, as if the wind has taken them and is about to lift them from the earth. He watched her approach with pleasure. The man followed her, walking, and holding Jinny's hand, but Davy was skidding across the grass and yelling with delight.

She stopped before Byrne, her face flushed, her breasts rising and falling, and her eyes bright. He too was embarrassed. Davy was pulling at his hand and shouting his name, and the Negroes, their emotions responding warmly to the boy's, gathered in a half circle, bobbing their heads and grinning until Byrne shouted at them to unsaddle.

When he faced her again she had one hand pressed against her heart and her lips were parted. 'I didn't expect you. Not soon. Not so soon as this.' And she smiled like a child.

Jinny pushed past her mother with her face uplifted and eyes closed, and Byrne raised her in the air as he had done before, and kissed her on the mouth. The child kicked and squealed.

'Reuben . . .' said Anne Norvall, turning to the man. 'Mr Byrne, this is my brother Reuben. He got back from Texas yesterday.'

The man was not much more than a boy, perhaps twenty-two or twenty-three, a blond boy who had his sister's eyes without their frankness. He took off his hat and wiped his sleeve across his forehead before shaking Byrne's hand. His thick hair was slicked back and it curled at the nape of his neck. He had a fleshy mouth over which drooped a frontiersman's moustache. But this did not seem at home on his face, rather something he had grown because he wished to be taken for a frontiersman. He had an old revolving pistol pushed into his waistband, and when he had greeted Byrne he put a hand on its butt, his body falling into a faintly melodramatic pose. Then he stared at the Negro troopers with that old familiar expression.

Anne Norvall looked over Byrne's shoulder to the bluffs. 'Where are the Indians?' she said, and when he told her she bit her lip, and her hand went instinctively to Jinny's shoulder.

'There's nothing to fear,' he said, 'I believe that they have gone on to the Plains, or perhaps into Texas. We've lost their trail.'

The brother spoke, jerking at the butt of the pistol. 'Comanches...?' he said, and he turned to her, suddenly angry. 'You see? Like I said, it's crazy to stay here.'

Byrne tried to reassure them. 'Even if they came, I'm sure they wouldn't harm you. Quasia's fond of the boy.'

'Comanches ain't like us,' said the boy aggressively. 'Maybe you're new to this country, mister.'

'No,' said Byrne slowly, suppressing an impulse to box the boy's ears, 'I'm not new, and perhaps I don't understand Indians all the way. But I don't think Quasia would harm this place. No one here has done him any injury, and, as I said, he's fond of Davy.'

'We're pulling out,' said Reuben to his sister. 'Ain't no sense in relying on the soldiers. We're pulling out tomorrow. You got a reason not to stay now. We'll go to San Anton'. I got friends there, I got a chance at a piece of land.'

'We've got a piece of land here,' she said.

The boy turned to Byrne. 'You tell her, mister.'

But before the lieutenant could speak Anne Norvall put a hand on his arm. 'You'll make yourself to home?' she said. 'How long are you staying?'

'Until tomorrow. Until I know where they've gone.'

'You'll come down to supper? I'd like you to come down to supper with us.'

He nodded, and she went back to the house with Jinny, her back straight, and her walk long and forceful, almost like a man's. Her brother remained, and he faced Byrne with his feet astride, and his right hand still resting on the butt of the gun. 'You can tell me, mister,' he said. 'How bad is it?'

'They killed a party of hide-hunters. We found the camp. I'm sure they'll go into Texas, maybe there already. One of their friends was killed by the Rangers, and it's their way to make a vengeance raid.'

'I heard about that,' said Reuben. 'I came over with the Rangers. Big man in a lion-skin vest was their captain. He said these Indians had been akilling and stealing down in Montague County.'

'Not these,' said Byrne.

'Don't make no difference what Comanche it was that done it, does it, so long as some of them pay for it?'

'You've been in Texas for some time,' said Byrne.

'I don't follow your drift, mister.'

'It doesn't matter. Maybe your sister should go, if you're set on taking her.'

'I'm taking her. I'm all she's got now. Her man was too soft with her.' He turned, and swaggered a little towards the house. Then he stopped and came back, whispering, 'These niggers are all right, ain't they?'

'What the hell do you mean?'

Reuben shrugged his shoulders. 'I'm asking, they all the Army's got in this country to protect us settlers, them buffalo soldiers?'

Byrne felt a little sick. 'Make your meaning plainer.'

Reuben's tongue licked the end of his moustache. 'I figure it was plain enough,' he said, and went.

Nasthoe left before dusk, crossing the river at the ford, his shoulders hunched, his long legs hanging, and the feather nodding in his hat. He did not look happy, and he was not happy.

Supper was over and the woman placed the lamp in the centre of the table. With each movement the glass tears on its shade rang against each other. She was wearing a black dress that smelt strongly of camphor. It covered her arms and neck and there was a ruche of yellow lace at the throat, pinned by a cameo. Byrne wondered when she had last worn this brooch, when indeed she had last worn the dress. The austerity of it suited her, giving her fair hair and her well-boned face an unexpected beauty in repose, the weathered lines around her eyes and her mouth smoothed away by the lamp's light. She was inwardly nervous, he knew that from her silence. She was wondering if her dress and her behaviour matched those of the officers' ladies with whom she believed he was familiar, and upon whom his values must be set. He wanted to reassure her that this was not so, that most of his adult life he had known troopers' wives only, but he suspected that any comment at all about her appearance would embarrass her. He wondered what sort of man her husband had been. And he wondered that such a woman was the sister of the boy Reuben.

The presence of her brother disconcerted Byrne, and he sat a little stiffly at the table, saying little himself, but now and then looking at the woman in an unsuccessful attempt to draw her into the conversation. It was Reuben who spoke most.

'Ranger captain told me they raided close to a mile from Gainesville last winter. The Comanches. In a blizzard the Ranger said. Captured a Mrs Shegog, he said, and Lizzie and May her girls. Said they chased the Indians clear over the Red where the Indians just laughed at them, on account of knowing that the Army would protect them.' He looked at Byrne, but the lieutenant said nothing.

'There was a Mrs Friend over in Legion Valley,' said Reuben, 'they shot her through with arrows and then scalped her, but she got up and walked a mile, mile and half to a neighbour name of Bradford. When he went across to her place in the morning he found they'd cut her youngest boy's throat. What you figure on doing with these Indians when you catch them, Mr Byrne?' He looked at the lieutenant in a challenge across the rim of his cup.

'I'm not an executioner, Mr Scott, if that's what you're asking.' He was angry with the boy's lack of perception. 'Do you think your sister wants to hear things like this?'

'Annie's got to know these things. She's got to see she ain't safe here.'

'It's all right, Mr Byrne,' said the woman, and she smiled tolerantly at her brother, 'Reuben's always trying to scare me.'

'Ain't trying to scare you,' he said sulkily. 'You ain't never

99

seen what's in front of your nose, Annie.' He pushed his cup away from him and stared at it before he looked up at Byrne. 'Rangers say the best thing is to kill every Plains Indian that sets foot off the reservation. That way things'd be safe for settling.'

'I guess it might,' said Byrne, 'but it wouldn't be very safe for the Indians.' He saw a twitch of a smile at the corners of the woman's mouth.

Reuben flushed. 'I guess you have been around nigger soldiers too long to know how white folk feel.'

'Reuben!' The woman's anger surprised Byrne, and he thought for a moment that she was about to slap her brother's face. But she took his shoulder and shook it as if he were a child.

He pushed back his chair to be free from her.

'Let me alone, Annie.'

'You tell the lieutenant you're sorry, right now, you hear?'

Byrne stood up. 'No,' he said. 'The boy's entitled to believe what he likes. And I must go back now.'

She stood up too, her back to her brother, and she said hesitantly, 'May I walk a piece with you, Mr Byrne?'

He was surprised, but he was pleased, and he opened the door for her, his hat in his hand. He heard the children's voices calling a good night to him from behind the gunny-sack curtain, and then he and the woman were outside the house. The moon was waning, but there was still light on the water, and the rise of grass on the opposite bank was like a drift of snow. She said simply, 'I was afraid you'd never come back.'

'I'm going to disappoint you,' he said. 'I should have told you when you asked. There are no women at Sill, not yet, and I've nothing to tell you about the things you wanted.'

'That wasn't the reason,' she said. 'I guess I was just worrying about you.'

'I worried about you,' he said, 'with more reason. It seems wrong for you to be here. Not because of the Indians, but it's lonely for you here.'

They were walking slowly towards the bivouac, her dress rustling stiffly. 'I haven't known much more than this. I mean living on the edge of things and such. My folk settled up in Indiana and then moved on to Minnesota. Paw always figured things would be a bit better further west. Seems like he was always working at things just to leave them. Maw used to say her children would never know how people lived in big towns, and Paw'd say who wanted to know?'

He thought she was using him as an excuse for speaking aloud thoughts that had remained silent too long, and he was moved by the compliment. 'Once,' she said, 'there was some Dutch settled ten, fifteen miles over from us in Indiana. They had lots of kids, and at Sunday meetings the kids used to talk about boats and such, crossing the sea, and when you got to understand the funny way they talked English, you couldn't find anything to tell them that was as good. They were always talking about what they'd seen.'

'It was because they were lonely,' he said, remembering. 'I used to dream when I was a boy, always about the same thing it seems now. I used to dream of a white road, with a stone wall on either side of it, and going up and down over purple hills. And a big bog with the turf cut and built in piles that look like the mesas you see here on the plains. I'd wake up in the morning and cry because I knew I'd never see that road again, but I suppose when I was there I never really noticed it.'

'You want to go back there?'

'No,' he said, 'I was a child, and lonely, that's all. It was worse for my father. He loved Ireland, and he was never able to balance that love against his hatred. The odd thing was that while he kept the love to himself he wanted to pass on the hatred to his children. He taught us the old songs, the ones that came out of his Irish hate, like *Shan Van Voght*.'

'Can you sing it now?' she said.

'No, I haven't the voice for it.' But he knew that it was because he hadn't the hate, and he couldn't sing a song of hate against the English when the only one he remembered was a fine-looking soldier on a horse.

'What was the *Shan Van Voght*?'

'It's Gaelic,' he said, 'or so my father said. Words meaning

101

the old woman, and the old woman being a way of describing Ireland. When he explained it to me I laughed. I said it was silly, I remember, and he hit me across the head. It wasn't the blow that hurt, it was the look in his eyes.'

'Reuben told me about the buffalo-hunters.'

'There was no need for him to do that.'

'He says what he can to get me to leave. He's a boy, but he really frets about us. Was it that young Indian that did it, the one who told stories to Davy?'

'I think so.'

'It's hard to see how they can be like that,' she said, 'I mean talking to the boy and all, and then killing.'

'They're hard to understand, but maybe we should try.'

'Why?' she asked bitterly. 'I guess Reuben's right. They're animals. The Ranger captain, the one who came when you were here, and he came over a while with Reuben, he said the way to look at the Indians was like they're wild animals, snakes or wolves and such, and had got to go before folk could make something out of the land.'

'There's more than one side to them. You know how Quasia was with Davy.' When she said nothing he went on earnestly, 'Why should he be like that if it meant nothing?'

'They won't let us alone. Those people Reuben said were killed. It's not a way to live, always scared of them.'

'It's not easy,' he agreed, and he struggled to put the right thoughts into words. 'But they're scared too, and hating them is maybe no answer. That ends in belts made of their skins, or pickling their heads in alcohol for the freak shows.'

'If they're just animals,' she said, 'maybe there's nothing wrong in that.'

'Do you believe that?'

'I do when I think of what they could do to Jinny and Davy.'

'Quasia wouldn't hurt them. I'm sure of that.'

'How can you be sure?' she said. 'Are you sure because there's no one you really worry for?'

'Perhaps,' he said. 'Perhaps that's it.' They were close to the bivouac now, hearing the throaty breathing from the blanket rolls, the restless hooves along the horse-line. 'This is wrong. For now you must either walk back alone, or I must escort you.'

'It doesn't matter. I'll be all right. You'll be gone tomorrow, I guess.'

'If my scout returns.'

'Davy wanted to come down. He figures maybe you'd let him ride one of the horses. I said I didn't know.'

'He can ride mine. He'll be safe on it.'

'Good night,' she said, touched him on the arm, and went quickly away.

At noon a gobbling cry from the other bank, and Nasthoe stood there with his carbine raised. He was on foot, and his long-necked horse was drinking. He rode over at last and would not talk until he had eaten, then he said that he had found signs across the Red, the marks of Indian ponies and of shod horses which were probably those taken from the hide-hunters' camp. The Comanche had stayed in a grove of black oak, resting there for two nights, feasting on a deer and preparing themselves for a big raid. He had found black and yellow paint congealed in the dust, and a broad stone that had been used to sharpen their knives. They had danced too. It need not have been Quasia's party, Byrne thought, it might even have been Kiowas, and he put this to Nasthoe, who said nothing. He sat on his heels staring at Byrne, the grey spikes of his hair hanging on his cheeks and his shrewd eyes hidden in the shade of his hat.

'Nasthoe, you rogue, you've not told me everything.'

The Wichita was amused. His shoulders shook a little as he enjoyed Byrne's impatience.

'Speak up. There's no time. Understood?'

Nasthoe told the story slowly, relishing each incident and paying as much credit as he could to his own cunning. He had followed the river downstream for five miles or more on the south bank and then crossed to the north. He found, as he expected, the marks where the Comanches had come out of the water, and he followed the trail eastward until it went into the river again. Once more he crossed to the south bank and rode along it, to the east still, until he found the trail. The Comanches had backed their horses out of the water until they had reached the thick grass and then they had ridden to the south at great speed. Some miles later they had been joined by a single rider, an Indian, from the west.

'Who?' said Byrne.

'You wait. I tell.'

Nasthoe had followed the trail, and towards dusk he knew that he must soon reach the Indians' camp, for no Comanche war-party travelled at night. He looked for the highest ground, fixed its position in his mind, and waited for dark. He knew that before camping the Comanches would approach the hill in a circle, surround it, and slowly converge on its top. Then they could camp on the opposite side to their approach and leave a sentry on the crown of the hill to watch the way they had come.

When it was dark, Nasthoe hobbled his horse and walked in a wide arc, keeping to the low ground and dry washes, and stopping now and then to make sure the hill was where he believed it to be. When he finally reached the Comanches he saw that they were camped by water and had lit a fire. He crawled in close to them, from downwind so that he might not be scented by their ponies, for he knew that it was their custom to picket the animals some yards from their camp and use them as sentinels. When he told Byrne this he smiled smugly.

'Go on,' said the lieutenant.

'I go on. I tell.'

There had been seven men at the fire, which meant that, with the sentry on top of the bluff, there were now eight in the party, one more than those who, according to Mow-Way, had left the agency. There were twelve horses, including the three taken from the hide-hunters. Nasthoe did not think the white men's horses would last long under the strain.

'Never mind the horses, who was the eighth man?'

'Ohanaki. I see him.' Yellow-eared-horse, Quasia's brother from the Staked Plains.

The Comanches were finishing their evening meal, and Nasthoe waited. Despite the arrival of his experienced brother, Quasia had obviously been elected as the leader of the party. He sat with the sacred war shield beside him, and he carried the sacred pipe. The young men smoked the pipe gravely, after first offering it to the earth and the sky, and when this was done they began to sing and dance, making a lot of noise Nasthoe remembered with disgust. A band of women could have stolen the young fools' horses, they made so much noise. The dance was interrupted at intervals by Quasia, or Red-Buffalo, or Yellow-eared-horse. They held up their hands and recited the story of a great coup performed by them, swearing the truth of the story this way, 'Father Sun, you saw it done. Mother Earth you saw it done. Do not let me live until the winter if I lie.'

A coyote-call from the top of the bluff silenced them, and, thinking it wise to leave, Nasthoe had walked back to his horse and ridden away. He looked at Byrne and waited for the due compliments.

Byrne politely expressed his admiration and gave the old man some tobacco, but he was disturbed by the news. His orders had been to intercept Quasia's party before it crossed into Texas, and although he had always thought this unlikely the problem of what he should do when it happened had never before been faced by his plodding mind. Now it was there. Theoretically, he argued to himself, he should return, report what had happened and let the situation be handled by the post commanders at Belknap or Richardson.

He felt perplexed by the division of his responsibilities. It had not been this way when he was a sergeant. Then he had sat, and smoked, and waited for an officer to make the decisions and take the consequences, reserving the right to approve or disapprove without being forced to act upon his opinion. Yet he knew what he must do, and he knew that what he did would be motivated by principles rather than tactics, and he wondered how many military decisions were based more on the self-respect of the responsible officer than on his objective assessment of the situation. That Quasia and the others had gone on this vengeance raid was arguably his fault. Had he prevented Whip-Owner and Brown-Young-Man from crossing the Red River, then the latter would not have been killed, there would not have been that ridiculous attempt to arrest Quasia, the hide-hunters would still be alive, and the Comanches would not now be in Texas. Therefore it was his moral responsibility to bring Quasia back or kill him. This was the first time that the thought of killing Quasia had entered his mind, and he was surprised that he could consider it so dispassionately.

He called for Salem. The sergeant stood before him, looking down calmly, one long leg bent at the knee, his eyes dark and watching, as if he were one step ahead of Byrne's thoughts and was waiting, as a man waits for a laggard companion.

'We'll march in an hour,' said Byrne.

'Over the river, sir?'

'Over the river,' agreed Byrne coldly. 'Or do you wish to debate the decision with me?' Then, with an intuition unusual in him, he added, 'You think it's unwise to take the troopers over there on account of that run-in with the Rangers?'

'If the Lieutenant thinks so.'

'And you're thinking it, too, damn you. Why can't this command operate without us hiccuping every so often over the colour of the troopers' skins?'

Salem pulled on his gauntlets and straightened his body. 'Shall I get them mounted?'

'Sergeant,' said Byrne, 'what did your master call you when he found you as ornery as I do?'

Salem paused and looked at Byrne. He was almost smiling, as if, far from resenting the remark, he was enjoying the embarrassment it was going to cause the lieutenant.

Byrne flushed. 'I'm sorry. I withdraw that, Salem. But if I'd said it to Honesty or Crispin they would have laughed, and told me. Why do I know I've insulted you?'

'Maybe because I'm half-white,' said Salem coolly, 'and it's the white half of me you think you've insulted.' He saluted and left.

Byrne walked to the house to say good-bye, picking up Davy at the horse-line, where the boy had been playing, and carrying him down on his shoulder. Anne Norvall's face was full of pleasure when she saw them together like that. He put Davy on the ground, slapped a hand on the seat of the jeans, and watched the child run off to the corral. Then he crouched down beside the girl Jinny, crooking his finger and stroking her chin with it until she first smiled and then laughed, and then pushed her face into her mother's skirt. He stood up, and Anne Norvall said, 'You like them. And they like you.'

'I like them,' he agreed simply, and he smiled down at the child's eyes as they watched him from a fold of her mother's dress.

Anne Norvall handed him, tied in a neat roll, the shirt and socks and drawers which she had laundered for him overnight. She gave him some biscuits too, wrapped in store-paper. They were still hot, and he felt like a child himself, being sent off to school. He said so, and she laughed because of the look on his face.

'I guess you're all boys,' she said, and the ingenuous remark restored him to the present.

'Your brother is right, you know. I've thought about it. It would be best for you to leave.'

'If you say so,' she said. Her eyes went to the grave on the hill. 'But it don't seem fitting to leave him.' It was a moment before he realized she was speaking of her husband. 'He never liked being alone. He used to say one day we'd move where a man could be buried with his friends. I don't want to leave him out here alone. There's maybe no sense in staying, but there's no sense in going too.'

'It won't always be like this.'

'I'll be running away.'

He gripped her arm, more fiercely than he intended. 'Don't you understand? I could be wrong about Quasia.'

She looked down at his hand, but instead of releasing herself from it, she placed her own hand over it. 'You never told me your given name.'

'It's Garrett.'

'It's not a given name at all.'

'It was my mother's family name. It's a custom in Ireland to give it to the first son. A custom among the gentry, that is, and my mother would say she couldn't see why they should have all the pleasures.'

'Do you remember her?'

'Very well. She was tall, with fair hair like yours when she

108

was young. But her eyes were brown, though. She had a fine singing voice, and she wanted me to be a priest.'

'Do you think they'll come here again?'

'The Comanches? Perhaps. But they have Quasia's brother with them now, and I don't know what they'd do if he forced them to it.'

'You like Quasia?'

'I like him.'

'And you don't think he'd harm us?'

'I don't think he'd let you be harmed if he could prevent it, no.'

'Well, then . . .'

They were standing close together, her hands still over his and when he realized this he released his hand in embarrassment. Davy came back from the corral, playing on the whistle that Attucks had made him from a bone the night before.

'Why didn't you become a priest?'

He smiled at her. 'It would have been a mistake, don't you think?'

'But why?'

'My father opposed it. I was the only son, and he'd say the priests had always betrayed Ireland, although he was a good and devout man. They would quarrel about it, my mother and father, about my becoming a priest, and my mother died before they could agree.'

'And he wanted you to be a soldier.'

'No, that was my own idea. After I ran away from him.'

'Why did you run away from him?'

'To grow up. His hand was always on my head.'

She looked beyond his shoulder. 'Your men are on their horses.'

'I'd like to know what you'll do.'

'My brother wants us to go. I guess we'll go, but I'd like you to know where we've gone, what happens.'

'You could write to me at the post.'

She smiled with pleasure, and she put both hands on her cheeks suddenly. 'I'm colouring,' she said, 'like a girl.'

Davy pulled at the bottom of his pistol holster. 'You going to fight the Indians?'

'We're going to find them, anyway.'

'You want me to come along and help?'

'No, Davy, but you can do something for me. You look after your mother. You help your uncle look after your mother.'

The boy was disappointed. He pushed the lick of hair out of his eyes, and blew two mournful notes from the whistle. 'I always done that. It ain't nothing. You going to kill that Indian, the one with the stories?'

'Not if I can avoid it.'

'What's he done?'

'*Davy!*' said the woman sharply, grasping his shoulder. The boy looked at her with a scowl, thrusting his hands into the waist of his jeans and working his toes into the dust.

'Good-bye,' said Byrne, putting out his hand to her.

'Good-bye, Garrett.'

It seemed a cold and impersonal farewell, set against what was in his mind. He held Jinny and kissed the child on both cheeks, and he ruffled Davy's hair, and the three of them stood close together watching him as he mounted. Beyond them, Reuben leant on the rail of the corral, scowling and chewing a grass.

'Don't forget,' said Byrne, but what it was he wished her to remember he did not say. She wanted to call out to him, words of reassurance, but he did not look at her again until the patrol was mid-stream, and then he stood in his stirrups and turned his face, raising his hat. She watched until the land had hidden them.

At three o'clock, when the patrol was walking its horses in the oppressive heat, one of the troopers at point rode back to say that there were horsemen over the next rise, drawn up on the far side of a wash before a grove of trees. They were white men. Byrne recalled the other point man, mounted the patrol and moved it forward at a canter. When they reached the top of the rise he saw the Ranger troop below, a long line of men with the sun on their hats and their white shirts, their horses idly cropping. There was no movement from them as the soldiers came down, but when the patrol halted by the wash the Ranger captain and his sandy lieutenant put their horses down the crumbling wall, crossed the bed and climbed up the other side. Adams looked at Byrne with sour amusement, his lips puckered, and a hand hitting lazily at the flies before his face.

'Well,' he said at last, 'lost yourselves, Lieutenant?'

Byrne took off his hat and wiped his forehead. His thin hair was stuck to his scalp by sweat, and he felt tired and in no mood for the Ranger's humour. 'A party of Comanches from the Kiowa Agency at Sill crossed the Red a day or so ago. My scout saw them at camp last night, and their trail leads this way.'

'Is that so?' said Adams, staring. He turned to the other man. 'You hear that?'

'I hear that!'

'I believe', said Byrne stiffly, 'that my orders will permit me to assist you in rounding them up.'

'They will?'

Byrne put on his hat and pulled down the brim stubbornly. 'Captain, if prompt action is taken we can clear up this affair before they do any serious damage.'

'We can?' said Adams, leaning forward on his saddle-horn and pushing up his hat with two fingers.

'Salem! Take Nasthoe and scout on a mile or so.'

'Now hold on, Lieutenant!' said Adams, straightening his back. 'You're off ground and you're wasting your time.'

'I am?' said Byrne, momentarily enjoying the switch in question and answer.

'We met your hookey players this morning.'

'We sure did!' said the sandy man and grinned. He bent over and pulled two scalps from his rope-strap.

Nasthoe grunted and pointed to one of them. 'Ohanaki!' he said.

'What's he say?' said Adams.

'He's recognized one of them.' Byrne looked at the soft feathers in the other plait of hair. 'The second one belonged to a Comanche called Red-Buffalo.'

'That so?'

Byrne had to ask the question. 'Why do you do that? Why must you take their scalps?'

Adams shook his head. There was no mockery in his voice now. 'You're wrong, mister, I'll swear, whatever you're thinking. There's no fun in it, not for me anyways.' He looked at the sandy man coldly. 'We take a Comanche's scalp when he's dead, or hang him, or kill him in the dark, and he figures he ain't got no chance of making the next world. We do it to lower the ante on their chances of everlasting joy when they come raiding down here.'

'Thank you,' said Byrne.

'You're welcome.' Adams looked tired and defeated, and he wiped a hand down his face as if he were dragging the weariness from him. 'They've run back over the Red. They're all yours again, Lieutenant, but if you think you can stretch a point in that rule-book of yours we'll be glad to come over and help you any time.'

'Thank you, no,' said Byrne, his head up.

The Ranger nodded briefly and turned his horse. At the lip of the wash he halted and looked back, resting a hand on the rump and speaking with genuine concern. 'We ain't leaving the country. We'll be here a while if you need us.' He waited for an answer and received none. 'Yes,' he said, 'I guess you'll follow your rule-book. But they're young bucks and they act like they've got nothing to lose. We were too many for them, but you might be more their size. Be careful.'

'Thank you,' said Byrne again.

Adams nodded. 'It was a word of advice,' he said, and he raised a hand briefly and recrossed the wash.

Byrne turned the patrol northwards to the Red River. It rode at the trot for three miles before he realized that, however urgent his anxiety, there was no point in breaking the horses. He walked the patrol for an hour, riding erect, his face turned ahead, his right hand brushing his thigh. There was a halt for another hour when Cometoliberty was nearly pitched from the saddle by a broken quarter-strap. Byrne fretted while another was improvised, and to distract himself he ordered the packers to reload the mules, watching them with a cold cigar between his teeth.

'James?' he called.

'Yes, sir.'

'When we mount up, you sing. You've a good voice, boy, and I like to hear it.'

'Yes, sir, Lieutenant!'

Byrne lit the cheroot and they rode on. For half a mile there was no noise but leather and steel and the breathing of the horses. He sighed. *You damn fool, did you expect him to let you patronize him? Why did you ask him anyway?* And then Miles James sang.

> Jesus make the blind to see,
> Jesus make the cripple walk,
> Jesus make the deaf to hear ...

Four or five other voices, Attucks' among them, joined in the response

> Walk in, kind Jesus!
> No man can hinder me.

Byrne smiled, and did not know that he was smiling.

At dusk they came to a homestead five miles from the Red River, a sod-house and barn, an acre or two of ploughed earth, and the white smoke whipped from the chimney by the wind. The settler was a German who could scarcely speak English. He ran out of the house waving a gun, followed by his wife and two loose-jawed sons who had rifles too. He said, and it took Byrne some time to understand him, that the Comanches had gone by there that morning. It had not been easy to see them at first, there had been a thick mist, and he had taken them for Rangers, running out to welcome them. Then he saw the feathers, the painted ponies, the shield held by the leading Indian, and he ran back into the house, yelling to his sons to put up the shutters. But the Indians had not stopped, they had ridden on towards the river as if they had not seen the homestead at all.

He was an old man and tired, and he was desperately frightened, clutching the rifle tightly so that his hands would not tremble. He was trying to be brave in front of his family, and Byrne was sorry for him. The patrol stayed long enough to drink the coffee which the woman made. She brought it to their stirrups in a big jug, her lined face shadowed by the wings of her sun bonnet. Although Byrne was irked by the delay he felt that he owed it to the man.

The sun was setting when they reached the Red, and they found the water too deep to ford. Byrne sent Nasthoe into it, but it could not be swum, the current was strong and the Indian's pony went deep into quicksand and had to be pulled out on a rope. Then the storm broke and Byrne ordered camp. It rained for three hours, making fires impossible. The earth turned to mud beneath them, the picket-pegs were washed away and the horses had to be hobbled. None slept. They sat with ponchos about their shoulders, the rain pulling the brims of their hats, and their eyes staring white from the dark misery of their faces.

Byrne watched them unhappily. The nature of each man reacted instinctively to the discomfort. Salvation Calhoun swore unceasingly, the words whispering from his yellow face, and his body locked in lonely malevolence. The clumsy boy Cato Brown was terrified by the storm, his hand inside his blouse and fumbling at the beads of his rosary. Attucks was like a cornered beast, blacker than ever in the rain, his chin down on his breast, and his great fists clenched. The truculent little trumpeter Riddle chewed tobacco and spat yellow streams of disgust into the mud at his feet. Only the fat, soft Crispin smiled, lifting his face to the rain and wiping the water from his cheeks happily. Byrne was worried about the old man Nathan, and he went across to him once, standing before him and staring down at the pouched eyes, the composed lips, and the long delicate hands.

'Are you all right, Uncle?' he said, unaware that he was using the affectionate name. But Donethegetaway noticed it, and smiled as he nodded his head.

'Sir,' he said, 'Lieutenant. Uncle's fine. Ain't no call to fret none.'

Byrne remembered the day at the river, when he had

watched the troopers bathing and seen the whip-scars on the old man's back. He remembered that although Nathan's body looked frail it was in reality almost all bone and muscle, the hardened labour machine. Donethegetaway was strong, and there was something stronger still inside him that the misery of weather could not touch. When Byrne turned from him he saw Salem, and the sergeant was smiling, that same smile of ironic pride.

The sun dried them out when they rode on the next morning. They travelled westward with the swollen river rolling on their right. Before mid-day they sighted the red bluffs on the north bank by Norvall's Crossing, and there Miles James, who was out at point half a mile ahead and in sight of the ford, halted and began to wave his hat over his head excitedly. Ordering Attucks to bring up the patrol as quickly as possible, Byrne rode on at the gallop with Salem. They joined James, who shouted, 'Something's wrong!', and the three of them went into the ford together. The river was deep and the flow strong, and the trooper and the sergeant took their carbines from the buckets and held the weapons above the wash of water about their waists.

The house was quiet, the windows shuttered, and although Byrne cried, 'Hallo there in the house!' there was no reply. As they came, wet and shining from the river, Reuben appeared in the doorway. He ran towards them, shouting and waving. Five yards from them he fell on his face, his shoulders heaving and his fingers digging at the earth.

Byrne dismounted and gently turned him over. The boy was crying, his ridiculous moustache wet with tears.

She was sitting in the rocking-chair facing the door, her toes tapping the floor lightly as she teetered backward and forward. She did not speak to him, and he stood watching her, listening to the sound of her feet and the creaking of the chair, his wet clothes chilling his body. He was familiar enough with the expression on her face, although it was some years since he had last seen it, on the faces of recruits stumbling back from the first shattering impact of war. It was a face abandoned by all thought and emotion.

A wing of pale hair over her right temple was disarranged, where, in one desperate impulse, she had thrust her hand through it. On her lap and beneath her apron was Jinny. He saw the stiff and tiny legs, the dusty toes parted, a hand hanging down with the fingers closed. The apron was bloody.

He called to her softly, using her given name for the first time, but she did not answer him. Although her eyes looked into his there was no recognition. She breathed regularly and deeply, and the chair rocked to and fro. He put on his hat and left her.

Reuben was sitting on a broken rail, his head between his knees and his arms hanging. Salem was holding his shoulder, and when Byrne came and stood before them he saw that the sergeant's face was no longer masked by defensive irony but was naked in melancholy grief. Reuben had been sick, and he looked up strangely, more of a boy still behind the moustache. He clutched at the lieutenant's arm and began to gabble, a frothing spate of disconnected words and sentences, halted suddenly when he was sick again.

'Salem,' said Byrne, 'Will you go and sit with Mrs Norvall? Call me when she speaks, but don't touch the child.'

The sergeant licked his lips slowly. 'He says you told them that the Comanches wouldn't harm them.'

'All right,' said Byrne harshly, 'All right. Go to Mrs Norvall. She's shocked. You know, you've seen it before. Sit with her and call me quickly if you have to. Understood?'

Salem pulled his body together slowly and left, and Byrne stood with his legs astride and his hands on his hips looking down at the boy. 'Mr Scott,' he said gently, 'Can you tell me what happened now?'

Reuben wiped the vomit from his chin, spitting into the dust. He began to shake his head in disbelief, and it seemed to Byrne that he would never stop. Thirty yards away the troopers waited, beneath their hats and slack hang of their jaws and their dust-grey cheeks. Byrne shouted 'Attucks! Canteens and horses!' and he saw the files move away to the river. The horses walked stiffly, necks stretched, and he knew that he could push them no further that day.

Reuben clutched at his sleeve again. 'You told her they wouldn't hurt us. She stayed because you told her that!'

'I'm sorry,' said Byrne emptily.

'You're sorry?' said Reuben, and he laughed crazily, 'You're *sorry*!' And then, in snatches, in hysterical, obscene sentences, in words close to weeping, he told Byrne what had happened. He had seen the Comanches on the other side of the river, riding at the gallop along the bank close to the water, and when they reached the ford they stopped and cried out, their weapons raised. He ran to the house, shuttering the windows and barring the door, and it was only when he had done this, and the Indians were already across that he realized he and his sister were alone, that the children were still somewhere outside. Anne Norvall screamed, clawing at the door to unbar it. But he would not let her out, holding her about the waist, telling her that Davy would know what to do, that he was sure to take Jinny to the hide-hole on the hill. He told her that it was better this way, for if the Comanches got into the house at least the children would be safe.

Byrne wondered if the boy had really believed this at the time, if it were not in fact fear rationalizing cowardice, but he was immediately ashamed of the thought, not knowing what he would have done himself.

'Where *is* Davy?' he asked.

'Davy . . .' said Reuben.

The Comanches had gathered before the house once they were all across the river, six of them, walking their ponies up and down and talking among themselves. Their faces were painted black, and there were black circles and arrows painted on the flanks of their horses. Then their leader, a man with a red blanket trailing, rode close to the house, calling and holding up his hand. Reuben poked the rifle through the shutter and shouted a warning. The Comanche called again, words which Reuben understood. He called. *'OurFatherwhichartinheaven!'* and at that Reuben fired his gun.

'You fool!' said Byrne bitterly, 'It was a way of saying he meant you no harm.'

The bullet passed along the shoulder of one of the Indians, and Reuben saw the blood come. The Comanches rushed towards the house, but Quasia stopped them. Reuben was reloading the gun when he heard the children, and heard his sister cry out to them from the floor where she was lying. He looked through the hole in the shutter again, and saw Davy and Jinny running down the hill. They were not afraid, and although Jinny stopped by the corral and put her thumb in her mouth Davy went on towards Quasia.

Reuben yelled the boy's name, and he fired the gun again, hoping to scare the Indians, but it only angered them. One of them shot back, and the bullet struck the edge of the shutter. Another fired an arrow which hit the door, and Reuben heard it humming there. Now Davy saw that something was wrong, and he shouted to Jinny to run, but she stood there sucking her thumb. She had a bunch of petunias in her other hand.

Although Quasia still called and pointed to the west, the other Indians moved towards the house. Reuben fired at them as they swerved past, but he did not think he hit any of them. The man he had hit with his first shot was a fat and pock-marked Indian who now rode close enough to the house to touch it with his gun before turning away. Reuben saw Quasia bend down and pick up Davy with one hand, throwing the boy across his horse. Jinny still stood with her thumb in her mouth and the flowers dribbling from her hand. The pock-marked Indian leant towards her, and although she moved away instinctively he caught her dress and picked her up. He threw her into the air, catching her by the leg. He held her dangling, and as he rode past the corral he seemed to swing her against a post, striking it with her head. He carried the body for another ten yards before he released it.

Then the Indians went up and over the rise to the west and were gone.

Reuben shouted at Byrne. '*What the hell are you standing there for? Why don't you get after them?*'

Byrne did not answer. Heavy-footed he went back to the house. Anne Norvall was still in the chair, but it was not rocking now. Salem looked at the lieutenant and shook his head. Then he turned his face back to the woman.

'Salem,' said Byrne, 'Go down and unsaddle, and tell Nasthoe to scout their trail.' He sat down, pulling a chair close to the woman, so that when the shock passed she would see him and not be alone. He sat there for fifteen minutes, feeling that perhaps he should be doing more than this for her, but not knowing what. Once Reuben came, stumbling clumsily over the doorstep, his mouth open to speak, and he was halted by the expression on the lieutenant's face. He went away, and soon Byrne heard the clink of a spade from the hill. He heard, too, the sounds of the bivouac, the rattle of metal, a horse's sneeze, footfalls and the snapping of wood under flame. But he heard no voices.

When she recovered it was gently. She saw him and knew him, and she leant forward. '*Garrett!*' she said, and began to cry. He took a blanket from the bed and covered Jinny with it before lifting the child from her knees. He walked out of the house with the girl across his arms. The troopers watched him as he staggered aimlessly through the dust. It was the old man Nathan who took the body from him and carried it back into the house, laying it on the bed and sitting beside it, without tears.

Attucks brought coffee, troopers' coffee, black and acrid, and the woman took the tin cup and placed it on the table beside her. She thanked the corporal but she did not drink it.

When the grave was ready she stood up and put a shawl over her hair, and walked up the hill firmly. Reuben carried Jinny, his back straight, and he knelt to place the child in the grave which was very shallow because of the ledge of rock beneath the earth. Nothing was said. The words of committal, half-remembered, moved into Byrne's mind, but his mouth was dry and he could not repeat them. He saw Cato Brown with the rosary between his fingers and his head lowered. Byrne knew what the boy must be saying, but was unable to join him. The singing came suddenly from the gathered troopers.

> For I am a stranger with thee
> And a sojourner as all my fathers were
> O spare me a little, that I may recover strength
> Before I go hence, and be no more seen.

The voice was Miles James', and the woman smiled to him in understanding. She tightened the shawl beneath her chin, looked once at the grave as Reuben turned in the first spade of earth, and then she walked back to the house.

That evening Byrne faced the woman's grieving indifference and the boy's anger. Reuben wanted to join the patrol. The Comanches had not taken his horse, nor the old grey, both having broken out of the corral when the Indians went through. Virgil Conception, looking for berries, had found them beyond the bluff at dusk and had brought them in. He would ride his horse, said Reuben, and join the soldiers in the hunt, and he looked at Byrne stupidly when the officer asked him what he thought his sister would do alone. Anger, hate and perhaps shame made it impossible for the boy to think with common sense.

'You told her they wouldn't hurt us!' he said foolishly.

'I know,' said Byrne. 'You can do what you like about that later, but now . . .' Reuben must take his sister to Sill when the patrol left in the morning, and they must travel quickly, even if they killed the horses in doing it. The patrol would bring back Davy.

'*Davy . . .!*' said Anne Norvall.

'I shall bring him back.'

'He's dead,' she said.

'No. I swear it. We'll bring him back!'

She sat all night in the chair without sleeping. Byrne handed his watch to the picket-line sentry, with instructions to pass the word that he was to be roused every hour. And every hour a gentle hand grasped his shoulder. He opened his eyes to see a dark face, and a soft voice said, 'On the hour, Lieutenant.' Then he went down to the house and stood in the open doorway. Each time he saw Reuben Scott at the table, his head on his arms and his hair falling over his fingers. Anne Norvall sat upright in her chair with her hands in her lap, and although she saw Byrne and recognized him she said nothing.

At dawn he went up to the rise where the last sentry of the night, George Honesty, was crouched, his carbine upright between his knees. Byrne put a hand on the trooper's shoulder when the boy began to rise. 'What do you see, bub?'

'Nothing, Lieutenant, 'cepting the sun coming.'

The horizon was red in the east, but Byrne looked westward for Nasthoe, and saw only the clear rim of grass against the pale sky. A meadow-lark was surging upward in song.

'Lieutenant, sir . . .'

'What is it?'

'We going back to Sill, now?'

'What do you figure we *should* do, bub?'

Honesty's amiable, stupid face was perplexed. He opened his mouth, scratched both cheeks vigorously and grinned.

'Do your duty, boy,' said Byrne, and went down the hill. He saw Anne Norvall at the grave, kneeling, her brown skirt spread about her. She was laying flowers on the fresh earth. He was surprised to see that Miles James was there, too, standing with his hat in his hand. As Byrne watched, the Negro helped the woman to her feet and held her arm by the elbow to escort her back to the house.

When the trooper returned to the bivouac Byrne called to

him. The man's habitual expression of melancholy understanding was more marked then ever. 'What were you doing over there?' said Byrne, aware that the question carried a disapproval he did not feel.

'Sergeant Salem sent me, Lieutenant, sir, but I was going anyhow when we saw her come out. She looked lonesome.'

'Thank you. That song you sang, James. At the burial. What was it?'

'One of the sweet psalms of David, sir,' said James in surprise.

'Thank you,' said Byrne, and repeated it in embarrassment, 'Thank you, boy.'

He had no taste for breakfast, and the coffee, scented by the smoke of the fire, burnt his throat, but he sat by the fire for an hour and fretted, until the sentry hailed and waved his hat. Nasthoe was coming, wearily, body slumped and his hat pulled down over his ears. When he dismounted he nodded to Byrne affably, saying 'Eat.'

'Nasthoe,' said Byrne firmly, 'We have no time to waste. I want the whole of it, now. You talk while you eat.'

The Wichita was disappointed and he shrugged his shoulders surlily. The Comanches, he said, had left a trail a woman could follow. It led toward the Staked Plains, and it was obvious that they hoped to lose themselves there, or find Quanah Parker and the other Kwahadis.

It was what Byrne had expected, yet the news was depressing. He knew that there were perhaps two thousand Comanches, men and women, scattered in small bands across the Plains under the loose leadership of Quanah, claiming the land as theirs still, raiding far into Texas and New Mexico, taunting the Indians who had taken the white man's road. If Quasia joined any one of these bands there would be little chance of finding him, of recovering Davy.

As he watched the Wichita eat, Byrne's mind slowly wrestled with the problem. It was not inevitable that young warriors, leaving the reservation by choice or expediency, should join those already on the Plains. Comanches preferred to live in small groups, and any leader allying himself with a

larger band would have to abdicate his position. It seemed unlikely that Quasia, proud and jealous, would wish to do this.
More probably would he endeavour to attract other young men
to him, and seek the protection of others only if necessary.

Byrne had never been to the Staked Plains. He knew of their
bitter reputation, and he had spoken with men who had cam-
paigned there during the second winter after the war, when six
companies of the Third Cavalry, a company of infantry, four
howitzers and a group of Navajo scouts had unsuccessfully
pursued the Cheyennes along the old Albuquerque trading-road.
Such men had talked with hate of the treeless wastes, the
waterless miles and the lonely mesas, and while it was true
that they had been there in winter they were sure that in
summer a man would find the land worse to endure. None
asked themselves how, then, the Comanches survived on the
Plains, for the Indians were animals and would slit open the
belly of a horse and drink its water before dying of thirst.

'We go back?' asked Nasthoe confidently.

'No,' said Byrne, 'We go after them.'

'Because of boy?'

'Because of the boy. And because of the girl too.'

'Girl dead. We dead too, for damn-sure.'

'Because of the girl,' said Byrne.

Nasthoe shrugged his shoulders and began to pinch the edge
of his jacket in search of lice. 'You damn-fool,' he said, 'I go
back.' But it was not a decision that prevailed against the argument of one of Byrne's cheroots.

Reuben had saddled both horses, and he and Anne Norvall
stood by them now as Byrne went down to the house. He did
not know what to say to her, and he was aware that because of
this his voice sounded rough and unfeeling. He asked Reuben to
take a report to Sill, addressed to Grierson, not Alvord.

To Colonel B. H. Grierson, U.S.C.,
Commanding Post,
Fort Sill, Ind. Terr.

Sir: The hostiles under Eagle-Tail-Feather have gone into the Staked
Plains. Yesterday they raided here, killing a young child and taking

123

a boy of ten captive, both children of Mrs Anne Norvall. I propose to follow and engage.

G. A. Byrne, Lt
Norvall's Crossing, I.T.

When she was mounted, sitting astride the grey horse, her skirts pulled up and her small feet in the stirrups, he put his hand over her wrist and said, 'I'll find Davy.' She turned her hand so that her fingers grasped his, but she said nothing.

'Don't stop,' he said to Reuben. 'Don't stop for anything. You should be there by tomorrow.'

The boy nodded, gathered the reins and kicked his horse forward. His sister followed him. She did not look back, or up the hill to the broken sunflowers and the two graves, but when she had ridden a few yards only she pulled at the horse and turned it about clumsily.

'*Kill them!*' she shouted, '*Kill them all!*'

The patrol moved within the hour. At the walk, at the trot, at the walk and trot again. Northward and westward. The mules had been loaded with flour, salt, bacon and beans from Anne Norvall's shelves. Ten miles and three hours from the crossing they came to the badlands, hard rock and red earth whipped clean of grass by stinging dust. Now they walked at the bridle to relieve the horses, their neckerchiefs pulled over their faces. Their feet stumbled and they walked oddly, left shoulder thrust forward and right arm pulled back by the reluctant animals. All afternoon the land mocked them, even when they left the badlands behind and moved first through razor-edged bunch-grass and then on to unbroken plain. The wind was a draught from an open furnace, caking their cheeks and the flanks of the horses with salt.

Byrne knew that Nasthoe had lost the trail in the badlands, where the eroding wind changed the shape of the earth even as they watched. Perhaps he had never found it in the beginning, but had trusted his own cunning, his intuition, his belief that Quasia must surely have ridden to the north-west in search of the great canyon which, said Nasthoe, split open the plain for fifteen miles. It was deep, he said. Two hundred tall men might climb upon each other's shoulders and still not touch the top. It was filled with cottonwood groves, cedars, wild china and hackberry, garlic, mustard and bluebonnets, green grass meadows and sweet water. There, twelve thousand ponies had once grazed while their owners rode a thousand more. There, the *comancheros*, Mexican traders from the Rio Grande, still exchanged rifles and ammunition, blankets and whiskey for the cattle which the Comanches stole from American settlers. On its red and yellow walls the wind had cut the faces of strange men and women, the heads of wolf and buffalo.

It sounded like a dream, and probably was, Byrne decided. He said, 'Have you seen it?'

Nasthoe shook his head. 'Many Comanches.'

'Will Quasia go there?'

'Not know.'

They found water at dusk, a stream running indifferently northward to what Byrne thought must be the Canadian, but how many miles away that river was he had no way of telling. The set of the sun revealed a long tableland in the far west, an indigo pencil-stroke between the red of the sky and the yellow grass. Nasthoe looked at this and nodded and would not say why. Watching the greasy head bobbing, Byrne was suddenly conscious of his mad dependence on a vain old man who had never been on this land before, but who followed some invisible map that had been drawn in his mind by half-truth, legend and imagination. Whether it was madness or not scarcely seemed to matter now, they must trust Nasthoe, and an awareness of this had put a sly swagger into the Wichita's manner, an insolence in his voice.

The water of the stream was yellow, and harsh with gypsum. Two of the troopers, Conception and Honesty, were sick from it that night, retching and coughing and staring at Byrne with sad eyes. He told Attucks, whose rank made him commissary to the patrol, to boil the water before canteens were filled in the morning, but he doubted whether this would be of any value. At dawn there was little dew, and the grass was so dry that it could be crushed to dust between thumb and forefinger. The horses refused to crop it, and fed from oats while their hooves were being plugged with clay. The sweat of animals and men smelt sour and strong.

When mounted, the troopers looked at Byrne, and the trust in their eyes disturbed him. 'Which way?' he said to Nasthoe.

The Wichita pointed to the tableland, now hidden in the morning haze.

'You lost the trail yesterday, admit it.'

The old man was hurt, and he picked his nose surlily, and rode off alone to the west.

'Salem,' said Byrne, 'Pistol practice for five minutes every hour.'

The sergeant raised his eyebrows. 'Firing?'

'No, drawing and aiming. You understand, don't you?' said Byrne, wondering again why he always thought it necessary to explain to the man. 'It will take their minds off the march.'

At first he saw no reason for sending men out to point, the grassland appeared to be so flat that an approaching horseman would surely be seen for miles. But the country deceived him, he found that it was scored by deep and hidden breaks in any of which a company of cavalry could remain hidden. The possibility of an ambush, of the Comanches rising suddenly and terribly from the brown grass troubled him, and he put riders out to the right and left, five hundred yards ahead. He changed them every hour, because he believed that in the unrelieved monotony of country such as this sixty minutes were long enough to expect a man to remain watchful and alert.

An hour after leaving camp he turned from the head of the column and rode beside it. His throat was dry and his voice was pitched high. 'Pistols,' he said. 'At the command *Raise!* you will unbutton your holster flap with the right hand and grasp the butt, back of the hand to the body. At the command *Pistol!* draw the weapon from the holster, reverse it with the muzzle up, holding the stock with the thumb and last three fingers, little finger under the butt, back of the forefinger against the trigger-guard. At the command *Aim!* point at...' His eyes searched the waste for a mark and saw nothing but the flankers. 'At the command *Aim!* right-hand men point at Cometoliberty out there, left-hand men at Calhoun. Any fool who pulls the trigger can buy the target a new hat.' The laughter was more than dutiful, and it pleased him. '*Raise!*'

He continued the drill for five minutes. An hour later he began it again, an hour later again, and again, and the troopers caught some humour from its inevitability. As he drilled them he watched them carefully, critical of them yet admitting to himself that they were not the same men he had taken out of Sill on the buffalo hunt. They were not perfect, but they were better, and if a cavalryman was not just someone who could sit a horse without falling off, to be able to do so was at least a beginning. When at last he discontinued the practice he nodded to them and smiled briefly. 'Good,' he said.

That evening at dry camp he knew that he had to make a decision. The patrol could not ride westward indefinitely, on and on until it found Nasthoe's miracle valley. He knew that he had perhaps gone too far already. They were not even following Quasia's trail, but searching for it in this bleak country, as uncertainly as a hand might feel for the wall in a dark room. There was no thought in his mind of returning to Sill, only an obstinate desire to come up with the Comanches as soon as possible. All day they had seen nothing, only the wash of grass and the white skulls of buffalo.

He went over and crouched on his heels before Nasthoe. 'When?' he said.

'Tobacco?' said the Wichita.

Byrne gave him a cheroot reluctantly, for he had few left, the Indian bit off an inch of it and put the rest inside his shirt. He chewed thoughtfully, yellow saliva running down his chin.

'Where are they, Nasthoe? Where are the Comanches?'

'No know. We go back.'

'You're thinking that, are you now?'

Nasthoe nodded vigorously. 'Damn-fool thing. Damn-fool country, damn-fool buffalo soldiers, damn-fool you, damn-fool Nasthoe. I go back.'

'Deserters are generally shot, old man.'

The scout grinned slyly. 'No shoot me. All Wichitas then make war.'

'The hell they would! They wouldn't miss you.'

'Out here die of no water, die of sun, maybe die of too much Comanche. Better shoot. You shoot.' He pulled open his shirt and grinned again.

'Damn your jokes, Nasthoe! Give me an answer.'

The Wichita scratched the back of his neck, and spat carefully between his moccasins. 'Old Shot-in-the-foot damn clever boy.'

'He's a wise old man, there's no denying it. Now answer.'

'Maybe north. We go north see *comancheros*.'

It seemed a sensible suggestion, and a little obvious, for it had been in Byrne's own mind for some time. If they turned to the north they might strike the Canadian, or the old Albuquerque trading-road and there find *comancheros* who, if they had not seen Quasia themselves, would surely have heard news of him. 'We'll go north, then,' he said.

'Go back,' insisted Nasthoe. 'Go back Fort Sill, get drunk.'

'No.'

'Damn-fool patrol this,' said Nasthoe.

Byrne talked with Salem, remembering how young lieutenants had once talked with him when he was a sergeant, using him as a reason for arguing their thoughts aloud, and not caring one way or another for his opinion.

'The Lieutenant wants to go on?'

'You know the situation, Salem. Quasia is in this country somewhere, and the boy is with him.'

'It's a big country,' said the sergeant, lifting his head and staring into the darkness with his calm eyes. 'It's an easy country to hide in, and easier still if you're only being followed by green cavalrymen.'

'How are the troopers?'

Salem smiled. 'The Lieutenant surprises me.'

'Damn the high-toned talk, Salem!'

'You're commanding a patrol of ten ex-slaves, all bred to obedience, sir. I'd say you're luckier than if you had white troopers. You'll get no argument from these men, they trust you.'

'Trust me?'

'Maybe not *you*,' said Salem softly, 'but the white man in a blue coat, the same white man in a blue coat that made them free.'

'Why do you despise them?'

'I don't, Lieutenant. I thought you were smarter than that.

But they are going to need you, and I'd like to be sure you aren't going to destroy them.'

'And because you think I will,' said Byrne bitterly, 'that's why you hate me.'

'I don't hate you, Lieutenant,' said Salem patiently, 'but I do love these men.'

'All right. You love them. I'll make soldiers out of them.'

'Yes, sir. You're going on after Quasia?'

'I'll find him. I've got to.'

'Because you want to kill him?'

'I do?'

'Don't you know that you do?' Salem stood up. 'Is that all, Lieutenant?'

'That's all.'

Byrne could not sleep. He put more chips on the fire, and crouched by it with his blanket over his shoulders. He took the notebook and pencil from his pocket, and looped his spectacles over his ears.

A commander must make decisions without emotion. A week ago you were capable of this. Not now. Why? What's the emotion? Hate? What do you hate? The Comanches? The negroes? Yourself?

Yes, you hate the Comanches. You liked and admired Quasia. You stopped the Rangers from killing him. Now *you* intend to kill him. Why? Because of Jinny and Davy. But you knew before the Comanches did these things. But you'll kill him. Because she asked you? No, because you want to.

You don't hate the troopers, you never did. You never liked them because you resented the fact you weren't given a white command. Now you're no longer sure they can't be as good as white troopers. Some you like. Like very much. Attucks. James. Old Nathan. Crispin. And Salem? Salem thinks he is your conscience. Damn him!

Most men hate themselves. With good reason. What do you know about hate, you've never felt it before. It's oddly satisfying because it's positive. Like love, maybe. You don't know about love, or do you?

Byrne looked at his watch. He had been writing for an hour, pausing for minutes between words, between sentences, and when he had read what he had written he was a little ashamed of the childishness of this self-analysis, and annoyed by the need for it.

You were ordered to bring Quasia in. Were you ordered to kill your troopers doing it? How many dead troopers will Grierson consider fair payment? How many will you? All of them, or some? Which ones? Riddle? Attucks? Salem? What will you feel if you kill Salem in this? Grief? Will you feel grief for any of them?·

Go back. No, find Quasia and kill him. You must find the boy. Find the boy. Kill Quasia. Ask Anne Norvall to marry you.

He read the last sentence with surprise, scarcely conscious of having written it, and inclined to laugh now that he had. He tore the paper from the book and dropped it on the fire. Removing his spectacles, he looked up from the flames and saw that Salem, leaning on an elbow, was watching him steadily.

Early in the march the next morning, with the sun on the right of the column, one of the flankers rode back to report that he had found a line of white stones and some weathered wooden stakes ahead, evenly spaced at approximately three hundred yards and running east to west. When the patrol came up with them Nasthoe smiled, and said that they were *mojoneras*, and wasn't he a damn-clever fool? Byrne had heard of the *mojoneras*. He remembered that men who had been in this country with the Evan's column during the winter campaign against the Cheyennes had spoken of them, saying that they were markers put up by Spanish traders long ago to point a route across the high plains and determine a way to water.

The patrol followed the stones, whether westward or eastward did not seem to matter, but Byrne instinctively chose the latter. Within two hours water was found, a stream with lush grass at its edges and thickets of wild plum from which birds started nervously. To Byrne it seemed a miracle. The whole plain was miraculous, an ocean of grass moving against the far escarpments, and a wind rushing ceaselessly. There were signs along the water, marks of unshod hooves many days old, grass horse-droppings dried to dust, the grey blots of long-dead fibres, even the ruts of waggon-wheels. All of them were re-assuring in their inference that the patrol was not alone in this singing emptiness, and all of them were alarming because of the possible hostility of the men who had made them.

Nasthoe pointed to the east. 'Comancheros,' he said, 'Soon see.'

But the next day they met nothing. The land became ugly, broken by ridges of rock, and the wind and the dust were bitter. The horses had less than a day's ration of oats left, and at nooning this was withheld from them so that they might be forced to graze. The troopers were sore-mouthed from the monotonous diet, three of them complaining of ulcers on their gums. The water they drank cautiously from their canteens soured their stomachs. All of them had diarrhoea, and there were frequent, painful halts while man after man relieved him-self, and although in the beginning this was amusing it soon lost its humour. They rode with their bodies lifted from the saddles and their teeth clenched.

The mules were evil-tempered, laying back their ears and kicking at the approach of man. Byrne ordered the blinds to be put on them, and told the packers to rope them close, but the animals fought against the weight of the aparejos.

'Shoot them,' said Nasthoe. 'Eat. Taste good.'

Byrne knew that the advice was sound. Before long the mules would have to be shot and the aparejos abandoned, but he was reluctant to do it yet. A peculiar obstinacy made him determined to keep the patrol in order for as long as he could.

'Shoot them,' said Nasthoe. 'Damn-fool bastards.'

'No.'

'Eat. Taste good.'

'Hold your damned tongue!'

He worried about the boy Virgil Conception. The trooper's face was a sickly grey, and he rode with a fist thrust into his stomach and his body bent over it. Twice Byrne saw Salem drop back and ride beside Conception, putting an arm about the boy's shoulders and whispering to him. When it happened a third time Byrne turned out of the column, too, snarling in a rush of anger that surprised himself. *'Get back up the line, Sergeant, and let the man ride!'*

When Salem rode on, his face unmoved, Byrne spoke gently to Conception. 'You all right, boy?'

'Yes, sir, Lieutenant.'

'Get your thoughts off it, if you can. You got something else you can think of?'

'I been thinking, Lieutenant. I been thinking of cool melons.'

'Glory be!' cried Attucks.

'Ride the horse all the way, boy,' said Byrne, 'You're doing fine.'

There were more alternating moods of anger and gentleness as he drove the patrol forward through the afternoon sun. He turned out of the column once to swear bitterly at Cato Brown who bounced unhappily in the saddle like a ball on a table. Then Byrne abruptly changed both his temper and his tone, riding beside the boy for five minutes, coaxing him softly. 'Grip with the knees, ride with the knees. Have you never straddled a tree at a swimming-hole, boy? Grip with the knees ... Left hand high, right hand hanging. That's it, that's it, bucko! Move with the horse. Move with it. Understood? That's it, that's it! You're doing fine, boy, fine ...!'

Alone at the head of the troopers, sweat chafing the flesh beneath his arms and inside his thighs, his hat brim pulled low over his broken nose, he stared forward at the face of Quasia. He saw clearly the round Mongolian face and the black eyes, the smoke rolling between the thin lips. Sometimes too, he saw the yellow horse, with slit nostrils flaring. He saw Quasia alive, and he saw the Comanche dead, on his back with eyes turning inward like the hide-hunter's, or the black-haired skull crushed like Jinny's. And when he could no longer look at these visions he turned out of the column again to upbraid or praise the sweating, swaying troopers.

Early, they passed the last of the *mojoneras*, but the trail eastward was plain, hooves, ruts, droppings, fire-stains and the marks of transient camps. Towards evening, with the thought of another dry camp filling Byrne's mind with dull anger, they

133

started a flock of ravens from the grass. The birds rose raucously from the earth, wheeled and flew to the east. Nasthoe was pleased. There must be men ahead, he said, many men, whom the scavengers were following.

'What kind of men? Comanches? *Comancheros?*'

Nasthoe shrugged. 'No tell. Too many sign.'

That night Byrne issued half a cupful of water to each man, ordering him to first moisten the mouth and nostrils of his horse before drinking what remained. The water and flour biscuits which the troopers made were like wood-dust, and Calhoun and Honesty would not eat, their cheeks puffed by the ulcers on their gums. Byrne took the brandy flask from the medicine pack, tipped it over the corner of each man's bandanna and told him to rub it on the sores. It seemed to ease their discomfort.

That night, too, the mules were killed and the *aparejos* burned. Nasthoe drank some of the water from the animals' guts and roasted some of the meat. He offered both to the troopers, and while they all refused the water most of them ate the meat, closing their eyes tightly as they chewed, as if to shut off the taste.

In his notebook, snatching at the memory of dimly remembered charts, Byrne tried to draw a map of the patrol's march. He estimated that they were perhaps eighty miles from Sill in a direct line, perhaps a hundred, a hard march of three days for men and horses in good condition. Then he left the notebook and his spectacles by the fire and went across to Virgil Conception. The boy had both fists thrust into his stomach, his body knotted, and the blanket tangled in his feet. He moaned, and he stank foully. Byrne gave him the last of his own water and sat for a while with his hand on the Negro's forehead until the boy's tortured body was still. Once more he saw Salem watching him intently.

He could not sleep when he went back to his saddle, and he wrote.

Is it the fifth day or the sixth? Conception is damned ill. Too young to be a trooper. Fourteen when Abe freed the slaves. Too young to die also. But I've seen white boys younger than this killing each other. No point in it. But if Conception lives will the rest of his life have any more point? That kind of argument makes you feel better, doesn't it? Why don't you borrow Cato Brown's rosary and say a few Hail Marys to make you feel better still?

You can't do it to men like this. Why? Because they are black? Because they were once slaves? You would do it to white troopers and call it line of duty. Are you being fair to white men if you think more of black troopers than white troopers? Damn them for being black and sitting on your conscience.

Go back. You can't go back and tell her you didn't kill Quasia, didn't get Davy. Go back. Kill Quasia. That'll make you feel better. Kill Quasia. How many black troopers is a dead Comanche and a live white boy worth?

Ten little nigger boys out on patrol. One got rot-gut and then there were nine. Funny.

He slept as he wrote, his body slipping down and the pencil and notebook falling from his fingers. He did not know that Salem got up and stood over him. The mulatto picked up the notebook, and when he had read what was written in it he placed it and the spectacles in the pocket of Byrne's blouse. Then he covered the lieutenant's shoulders with the blanket.

At dawn the last of the water was drunk, and by noon the patrol came up with the *comancheros*. Their camp could be seen three miles away and Byrne halted to stare at it through his glass. There was a ring of big-wheeled *carretas*, with a horse-herd to the north of it, and cattle grazing to the south. The sun shone on the bleached canvas of the waggons, on the white smoke pulled southward by the wind. Byrne ordered the flankers in with a wave of his hat, and he told Riddle to sound a call. The bugle brayed on a faltering note, for the trumpeter's lips were swollen and split, and when he took the instrument from them he wiped the blood from its mouth. He saw Byrne frowning at him, and he smiled. It was the first time the lieutenant had known the man to smile.

'Walk march, *ho* . . .!'

They saw men about the *carretas*, men in loose white shirts and wide hats, and they heard the sound of voices calling. There was a wild movement among the horse-herd, a swinging of ropes and an excited whistling. When the patrol was within half a mile of the waggons six horsemen spurred towards it.

The first was riding a fine black horse with silvered harness. He had a red and yellow striped *serape* over his shoulders, his head through a hole in its centre, and he wore a great straw sombrero with a needle crown. Although most of the other riders were bootless all were armed with repeating rifles, and they drew up in a line across the way of the patrol, the wind pulling at horse-hair and blankets. Their hostility and doubt seemed to fill the space between them and the troopers with uneasy vibrations. Although impatient with it, Byrne understood their suspicion. The Army's attitude towards the *comancheros* had never been clearly defined, but the Mexicans could be excused for not expecting it to be sympathetic. He raised the palms of his hands towards them in the plains greeting of peace, and held them there until the leading rider repeated the gesture.

The man then moved his horse forward at the walk and halted a yard from Byrne. He was extravagantly dressed in yellow buckskin and silver, a floral shirt of rippling colours, but he was old and wizened, part Mexican, part Indian, part Negro perhaps, a face darkened and twisted by sun and age. A circle of hair ringed his mouth and chin, and he picked his teeth idly with his little finger as he stared at Byrne. When he finally spat out whatever it was he found there he nodded to the lieutenant. '*Señor?*'

Byrne remembered. 'Salem!' he said, 'Use your Spanish. Say we would like some water to begin with.'

The *comanchero* laughed, opening his mouth wide. Most of the molars were missing from his upper jaw, and the black gaps they left were startling.

'*Cristo!*' he said with mock respect when Salem had finished, and he looked at Byrne ironically. 'Is he asking me for water, *señor?*'

'I hope so,' said Byrne stiffly.

'In Spanish?'

'That was the idea.'

'*Ay-ee!*' said the *comanchero*, 'Such education!' He laughed again, and turned his horse about, spurring it towards the waggons. He shouted '*Aguador!*', repeating the call until a man ran out with a goat-skin bag on his shoulder.

The *jefe* said that he was Don Cristobal Florencio Jorge Guaneros y Ruiz. He said this as if he did not care whether Byrne believed him or not, but was merely amused by the fertility of his own imagination. He repeated the name several times, enjoying the sound of it. He said that he was from Paso del Norte, which was probably true, and that he was a great *haciendero* there, which was probably not. He sat by the fire with his straw hat resting on the ground beside him, one of Byrne's few remaining cigars stuck in the side of his face, and his dark eyes regarding the officer with amusement. Beneath his good humour, however, there was uncertainty. He was still unconvinced that the patrol had not come there to arrest him. He had asked Byrne this quite bluntly, and had been so amused by the thought that he had burst out laughing without hearing Byrne's impatient denial. Still, the doubt remained.

Byrne knew that the man was a rogue, judged by the arbitrary ethics of the States. He sold guns to the Comanches and accepted payments in stolen stock. Byrne had seen at least four different brands on the *comancheros*' cattle. Yet Guaneros had been kind, and had himself lifted the boy Conception from the saddle and carried him to his own waggon, laying him beneath it and covering him gently with blankets. He had poured black powder down the sick Negro's throat, and then turned to his men and made a joke which, on the evidence of gestures alone, must have been foully obscene. He had filled the patrol's canteens from kegs strapped to the sides of the *carretas*, and had insisted that his own men water its horses. He had fed the soldiers on frijoles and fresh-killed meat, laughing at the grease shining on the dark cheeks. Now the Negroes were sleeping in their bed-rolls, their first night unbroken by sentry-duty.

138

But Byrne was anxious. Four times he had asked Guaneros for news of Quasia, and each time the *jefe* had taken the cheroot from his mouth, studied its wet end, and shrugged his shoulders. He seemed bored by the subject, but the boredom was too theatrical and too obvious, and there was a little fear in his eyes. For the fifth time Byrne asked about Quasia and now also he mentioned Davy.

'*Por favor?*' said Guaneros.

'A boy. An American boy. The Comanche has him.'

Guaneros put the cigar in the centre of his mouth, gripping it with his teeth, and drawing back his lips. He looked like a snarling animal, and it was obviously a trick of his, something he did when he wished to have time to think. Then, with one finger, he scratched the top of his head.

'*Señor*,' he said, unhappily, 'the Comanches are my friends. What they want I try to get. What they have I like to take.'

'These Comanches have a white captive, Guaneros.'

The *jefe* moved his head from one side to the other, almost laying an ear on his shoulder. '*Por favor!*' he said again and appealingly this time.

'*Señor*, I intend to recover the boy. Have you seen him?'

'A little one with white hair?'

'Where? And when?'

'A day, two days,' said Guaneros easily. He looked at Byrne. 'Why worry? The boy is all right, they will make a little Comanche out of him. It's better if his parents are dead.'

'His mother is alive. She wants him back.'

'Ah,' said Guaneros. 'Has she money?'

'She has no money.'

'*Lo siento mucho*,' said the *jefe*. 'What a pity.' He smiled at Byrne. 'I have not seen him.'

'That's no good, Guaneros.'

'No,' said the *jefe* sadly, 'I am always a bad liar.' He stared at Byrne gravely. 'You are sure his mother has no money, *señor*?'

'I told you. She has no money. Did you speak to the Comanches?'

'Of course. They wanted bullets. They had horses to trade, no good horses with lungs burst.'

'What about the boy?'

Guaneros leant forward, and he placed a hand on Byrne's knee. 'You understand? I would have traded for the boy if I could. The one called Quasia had no wish to trade him, but the others wanted ten horses for him, and guns.'

Byrne wanted to hit the man. 'And he wasn't worth it?'

Guaneros shook his head angrily. '*Por favor* ... Don't be angry. This is nothing new, the Comanches are always wanting to trade us captives. We could give away all our goods in one season and go back with what? A few white women and children whose relatives are dead or couldn't find a dollar for paying me? You understand?' he said, '*Esta claro?*'

'They will kill the boy now.'

'No,' said Guaneros. He tapped the ash from the end of the cheroot and eased his buttocks on the ground. 'Why should they kill him?'

'They killed his sister. They swung her head against a post, Guaneros.'

'*Lo siento mucho!*'

'His mother wants him back. I intend to get him back.'

'*No me gusta.*'

'Will you speak in English, please, *señor*? I want you to take me to them.'

Guaneros tugged angrily at his serape. He spat out a word that expressed his contempt for Byrne's innocence. They said nothing to each other, but stared at the fire until Byrne pulled out his watch. He unhooked it from the chain and held it out to the Mexican. Guaneros took it, opening the case with a dirty thumb-nail. He held the watch close to his ear, nodded approval, and returned it to Byrne.

'It's yours,' said the lieutenant, 'if you or one of your men will guide us to the Comanches.'

'So that you can kill them, *señor*? And then so their friends can kill me? All for a watch I do not want. I have a watch in the sky, *señor*. If I help it will be for nothing.'

'I apologize,' said Byrne.

Guaneros grinned. 'I help you for nothing because a watch is no good to me, and because the mother has no money. I am not a good man. I am very bad.' He grinned again.

'I'll be grateful for any help.'

'And you'll not try to arrest me?'

'I shall not try to arrest you,' said Byrne gravely.

Guaneros laughed loudly. 'Such comfort that is!' And then he was silent again, thinking, until he at last said, 'The boy wrote something.'

'He wrote something?'

'It is usual. The captives write to their friends and ask for ransom. I said the boy should write and they let him.'

'Give it to me.'

Guaneros narrowed his eyes. 'You are not lying, *amigo*? There is no money?'

'There's no money, only a mother, Guaneros.'

'Some mothers are bad. Mine was a witch. Maybe she beat him, maybe he's happy now with the Comanches.'

'Give me the note, or I shall take it.'

The threat amused the *comanchero*, but he fumbled inside his shirt and brought out a buckskin bag. His eyes half-closed against the smoke from the uptilted cheroot, he opened the bag and took out a square of folded paper which he gave to Byrne. On one side was a bill of sale for cattle in Taos, on the other were some crudely-printed words. Byrne held the paper close to the fire, but the flames had fallen and he could not see. Guaneros tore grass from the earth and dropped it on the embers. 'I told him what he should write, *señor*. There is a form for these things.'

'Put more grass on the fire, please,' said Byrne, but it was not the lack of light that prevented him from reading. Without looking at the *comanchero* he took out his spectacles, his fingers trembling as he looped the wire over his ears.

'*Muy bueno!*' laughed Guaneros. 'I have been a big fool. I should have asked for those instead of the watch.'

'It's no good,' said Byrne. 'Have you a lamp?' The glass of the spectacles was greased by thumb-prints, and he rubbed it on his blouse impatiently. Guaneros called for the lamp, and when it was brought he said 'The Comanches meant the boy no harm. I told you Quasia wanted to keep him, but the others said he was sick and would die, and should be sold.'

'He's sick?'

'*Esta bien*,' said the Mexican. 'Maybe nothing.'

Byrne pulled the lamp to his thigh, and held the letter down in its glow.

deer Frend who you are Can you by me of the Indans for ponnys my Maw lives at Norvalls Crossing on the Red where the Indians took me they kilt Jinny Rite her plees and send my riting Send money for ponnys to Mister Gwanos he is a good man Mister Birn at the fort is a good man to he is a soljer and noes me. Good by Davy Norvall aged 10 yeers

Byrne folded the letter and handed it to the *comanchero* who shrugged his shoulders. 'Keep it, *señor*. It is no good to me if there is no money.' And he smiled.

'Will you guide me to where you saw the Comanches?'

Guaneros shook his head. 'No, I have done enough. Go and get more soldiers. The Comanches will kill you and your blacks. They will kill the boy anyway if you find them. It's better to buy him, but you say there is no money.'

'There's no money, Guaneros. Can you let me have horses?'

The *comanchero*'s face was like the underside of a piece of leather, rough and dark, and even a well-intentioned smile seemed to increase its ugliness. 'Horses? For what?'

'Against a note I could give you.'

'Where should I claim it, *señor*? I should go to your fort and invite your soldiers to arrest me?'

'It would not happen that way.'

Guaneros shook his head. 'I could get double your price in Mexico.'

'Your price would be met.'

The Mexican was uneasy. '*Señor*, please understand. I do not ask the Comanches where they get the horses I buy. I do not look too closely at the brands, and I do not wonder why Indians should have shod horses. But your colonel might ask me why I have sold horses with this brand or that.' He shook his head.

'Then tell me, where might I find Quasia?'

'To the east, maybe, in the bad country. Two days.' He began to pick his teeth again, reflectively. 'What will you do when you find them?'

'I shall kill them all.'

'*Carajo!*' said Guaneros in disgust. 'Why? Because they live like they do? It is maybe a better way than yours and mine.'

'I shall kill them.'

Guaneros laughed. 'So small a thing, and who cares? You and your slaves and a few *barbaros*. Who cares whether you kill each other. I do not care.' The cigar had burnt down to his lips, and he spat it out. 'You have another *puro*?'

'No,' said Byrne, determined to keep the last for himself.

Guaneros seemed intrigued by the thoughts he had put into his own mind. 'In ten years, *señor*, there will be no free Comanche, no *comancheros*. There will be farms and railroads and bankers and men talking politics. They will not even care where your grave is or what happened to the boy. I do not want to see it, but it will come. Why hate so much? Nobody cares.'

'I care.'

'I tell you,' said the Mexican earnestly, 'you are a fool. This man is a Comanche, you think you can catch him with a few black slaves.'

'They are free men, *señor*!'

'Oh yes, I know. You had a big fight and killed each other and then the blacks were free. Have you whiskey?'

'No,' lied Byrne.

Guaneros grinned. 'I have a surprise for you, there is whiskey in your saddle-bag.' Byrne's angry face amused him. 'Don't be embarrassed, *amigo*, a man is entitled to the privacy of his own lies.'

'But not to his own property, evidently.'

'I did not take any. I did not look, it was one of my *bravos*. You are going to leave in the morning?' Byrne nodded. 'You stay another day, two days with me, then maybe your sick slave will get better.'

'No,' said Byrne. He stood up. 'I thank you, *señor*, for your hospitality and your help.'

Guaneros nodded. '*De nada*. You are sure the boy's mother has no money?'

'She has no money, but she will be grateful to you.'

'*El gusto es mio*,' said the Mexican ironically. 'It has been my pleasure. Good night.'

Byrne went to where Conception was lying. The boy's face was grey, and he lay on his back with his mouth open, his fists pressed into his belly. There was a rank smell of excrement about him. He opened his eyes when the lieutenant placed a hand on his shoulder.

'How is it, boy? How are you feeling?'

Conception said nothing, but there was a movement on the other side of the waggon, and Byrne saw that Salem was there, in his shirt-sleeves with a pan of water between his knees and a wet rag in his hand. He said 'Virgil couldn't stand on his feet, Lieutenant, leave alone ride. If you put him on a horse he will fall off, and if you put him back on he will die.'

Byrne looked down at the sick trooper. 'Where is he from?'

'Who knows?' said Salem bitterly. 'But he walked to Arkansas to enlist and there were no soles to his boots when he arrived. He figured that if he became a soldier the white men might teach him to read and write.'

'And did they?' asked Byrne harshly.

'No, sir, but he learnt a little from me. He can write his name and rank, his company and regiment.'

'It's a beginning, I guess.'

'Will the Lieutenant try to take him on tomorrow?'

'I don't know. Get some sleep, Sergeant. I'll sit up with him a while.'

They left Virgil Conception with the Mexicans. It was Guaneros' suggestion, but one which Byrne, sitting alone with the sick boy during the night had decided to make himself in any case. The *jefe* said that he proposed to remain there in camp for three or four more days and he would be happy to look after Conception. If the black died, he said equably, they would bury him, say a few prayers over him, and leave a marker on the grave. If he recovered then maybe he could rejoin the patrol when it returned, although Guaneros made it plain from the tone of his voice that he considered the patrol's survival unlikely. He was more blunt about this later, saying the boy was lucky to be sick now instead of almost certainly dead later. Life, he said, was a matter of varying misfortunes, and compared with his comrades Conception undoubtedly had the advantage.

Byrne left behind with the boy the weakest of the patrol's horses, and its saddlery. He took Conception's carbine, but left him his pistol, and he wrote a note and pushed it into the pocket of the trooper's blouse.

Private Virgil Conception, Company M. Tenth Cavalry, left behind sick by my patrol on the Staked Plains. It is requested that all possible help should be given to him to enable him to rejoin his regiment at Fort Sill, Ind. Terr.

G. A. Byrne, Lt, U.S.C.

They rode to the east, two hours after dawn. Byrne waited until the patrol had passed him before he moved to the head of the column. He saw the grey faces and the dirt, the ribbed-thin horses and the worn leather, the sole hanging down from Attucks' right boot, the rent sleeve of Honesty's blouse,

Calhoun's suspenders repaired with twisted grass. He saw these things, but he saw also something beyond the shabbiness, of which the only manifestation was perhaps the bright burnish of Riddle's bugle, the unexpected stiffness of Cato Brown's back. He felt the satisfaction of pride, and it didn't occur to him that a week before the appearance of these men would have filled him with disgust and despair. As he moved past them to the head of the column he did not look at them, but spoke out of the side of his face. 'Ride the horse all the way!'

Guaneros, the last of Byrne's cheroots twisting the corner of his mouth, rode with the patrol for a mile, silver ringing on the harness of his horse, and his short legs thrusting out the tooled flaps of his stirrups. He said nothing on the ride, but when he turned out of the column at last he took the cigar from his mouth and raised his hand.

'*Buena suerte, señor,*' he said. '*Vaya con Dios!*' The eyes in his nut-wrinkled face were curiously respectful.

The sun burnt the faces of the troopers all morning, even though they tipped their hats low over their noses. After they had nooned, it bit into the napes of their necks. Sweat stained the faded flannel on their shoulders, first black and then white with salt. The horses marched woodenly, heads jerking towards the earth, and the breath wheezing in their chests. Two of them were round-bellied and in need of a purge, and when a third lost a shoe towards evening Byrne ordered its rider to cut a slipper from a saddle-bag and tie on the hoof. They camped early, a dry camp in a sandy-bottomed wash, and as the sun set Byrne stared to the east and saw the harsh, red, hacked-tooth highlands ahead.

In the morning he drew the point men in to within two hundred yards, changing them every half an hour, and on the hour every hour he drilled the troopers in drawing and aiming their pistols for five minutes. This time it did not amuse them, and he heard the side-mouthed whine of Calhoun's protests. Nasthoe rode sullenly and silently, and when Byrne once sent him ahead to see if he could find the Comanches' trail he was back within two hours shaking his head. He was obviously afraid. He said that this was bad country and it promised to get no better. The hostile red escarpment seemed no closer than it had at dusk the night before, and the corrugated grassland before it contained scores of hollows in any of which a company of horsemen could be hidden. Nasthoe could not be expected to scout all of them, nor would have done if ordered, Byrne knew. The flankers kept appearing and disappearing like tiny boats as they rode in and out of the valleys. With each disappearance Byrne waited anxiously for the reappearance.

Towards evening they found water, an almost dry stream scarcely moving over a bed of flat white stones. But it was strong with gypsum, and remembering the agony of Conception the troopers did not grumble when Byrne ordered them to leave it alone. The canteen water was rationed sparingly, and when Byrne asked Nasthoe if they would find sweet water the next day the Wichita shrugged his shoulders and pulled his blanket about him. When Byrne sent him out to scout at dusk he went willingly enough, and unafraid, trusting to the dark. He returned after midnight, and he sat before the lieutenant like a shadow, his voice dry-throated. He had found Comanche sign, a day old perhaps, the picked bones of a horse that the Indians had slaughtered and eaten.

'Quasia?' asked Byrne.

Nasthoe thought so. Buried beneath stones he had found the shavings of a man's hair, probably that of Whip-Owner, still mourning for Brown-Young-Man. There had been other signs, too, that meant nothing to Byrne when he was told of them, but which satisfied Nasthoe.

Dawn was gentle, a mother-of-pearl haze and a great stillness in the air. Byrne stood by his saddle, rubbing his hands briskly over his bearded cheeks to bring life to them. He ate little, there was little enough to eat now, even with the jerked beef and hard tortillas that Guaneros had given them. It was not food that worried him, but water. His experience had been wide and hard, yet he had never before realized how soon water could be exhausted. He fretted as each man was issued with the third of a cupful, swearing desperately when a single drop escaped from the lip of a canteen to the earth. The lack of water showed in the troopers' faces, in the puffed and wrinkled lips, the dry grey skins, the movement of throats in search of saliva. He told them to suck pebbles. He smiled at them and lied, saying Nasthoe had promised water by nightfall. All day he repeated the assurance until in the end he believed it himself, and was scarcely surprised when, at nightfall, the Wichita did indeed bring them to water, a shallow stream free of gypsum. There was enough to water the horses, to fill the canteens, even to wash. He shaved, the blunt blade jumping over the long bristles, and he felt stronger.

But he knew that this was one stream only, and that within a day the canteens might once more be empty. Even so his spirit responded to the joy of the troopers. When Attucks asked if the troopers might give thanks for the water, Byrne nodded, and sat by the fire listening.

The corporal stood in the centre of the soldiers, his arms outstretched and his hat crushed in one hand. He lifted his black face and red-rimmed eyes, and the words throbbed from his mouth with great emotion.

'Oh Lord, Your people thank You . . .'

'*Amen!*'

'For bringing them to sweet water, they thank You . . .'

'*Amen!*'

'Oh Lord, who took Jonah from the whale and the Israelites from Egypt, Your people thank You . . .'

'*Amen!*'

'Oh Lord, Your people rejoice and praise Your name . . .'

'*Hallelujah!*'

And Miles James began to sing '*You read the Bible and you understand, Jonah was a witness for my Lord . . .*'

Salem did not join with the troopers. He watched them soberly, hands thrust beneath his suspenders, one knee bent, and his hat-brim pulled down over his face. Byrne got up and stood by him. 'The thanksgiving a little too simple for you?'

The mulatto turned his face slowly. 'No, Lieutenant. But maybe a little too premature.' He looked away again and said, 'We're going north to the Canadian tomorrow?'

'Is that what you'd do?'

'Does it matter what I'd do?'

'It might, Salem, if you have to command this detail.' The suggestion seemed to amuse the sergeant, and Byrne went on in a harder tone, 'We'll head for the Canadian if Nasthoe says the Comanches have gone that way.'

'They haven't,' said Salem, and he looked down at his boots, working the toe of one into the dust. 'They've gone into the badlands, thinking maybe we won't follow them there. Or maybe hoping we will. The lieutenant knows that,' he said, raising his eyes to Byrne's face.

'Then we'll go after them.'

'Yes sir. I thought we would.' He turned away.

'Salem!' Byrne called him back. 'Damn you, don't you know why?'

'I know why, Lieutenant, you don't have to tell me.' It was no answer, but Byrne let him go.

When Nasthoe returned it was to report that the Comanches had left many trails ahead, advancing and returning, and it seemed to him that they were anxious not to get too far ahead of the patrol. 'We smart,' he said. 'We go back.'

'Back where? They are between us and Sill.'

'Back. Back north. Find big river. To hell go Comanches and white boy.'

'Shut your mouth, Nasthoe, and do as you're told.'

'Damn-fool order,' said the Wichita. 'No ask to talk.'

In the morning Byrne was awake before dawn, before the picket-line sentry sang his soft reveille. The lieutenant lay with his hands clasped behind his neck, his eyes empty and his mind dwelling on the curious persistence of bird-calls in the east. When he could not identify them he at last stirred himself and walked across to the horses, recovering his watch from Done-thegetaway who was sentry there. The old man's face was more grey and melancholy than ever in the chill air, his arms crossed over his chest and his carbine cradled in them, but he smiled to Byrne. 'It's a fine morning, Uncle,' said the officer, and Nathan looked at the flush of day along the eastern horizon and nodded with gentle approval.

Byrne called the men himself, shaking them by the shoulders

until the blankets heaved and the air was filled with voices. A horse whinnied, and smoke thickened along the earth as dew-damp chips were dropped on the fire by Attucks. The sun thawed the man-smell and the horse-smell, and there was promise of the day's cruel heat in the thin haze. Byrne turned to the look-out that had been stationed on a low rise to the south-east. The last relief of the night was Riddle, sitting there now on his heels, his bugle bright between his shoulder-blades, his hat down over his eyes, and his hands gripping the stock of his carbine. He looked down to the wakening camp and then he looked to the east, and he stood up, his short legs astride, a hand shielding the sun from his face. Byrne heard the bird-calls again.

Riddle collapsed suddenly, the carbine falling away and the brass of the bugle splintering the sun. The sound of a gun-shot was very loud.

It immobilized the camp, the troopers staring across the stream to the rise and the dark clump of the trumpeter's body. Some were in their undershirts, others were bootless, and their mouths were open in stupid surprise. For a moment Byrne felt only anger with them for not sleeping fully-clothed as he had ordered, and then, as four Indians came round the rise at the gallop, he felt nothing at all and reacted instinctively. He called for carbines, and ran to the front of the troopers, falling on one knee with his pistol pointed at the approaching riders.

He saw Salem and Attucks dropping down on his right and left with their carbines raised. He heard the corporal shout 'Glory be!' He saw the muscles swelling on the chests of the Indian ponies as they came up the slight slope from the water. He heard the discharge of his own pistol and through the smoke of it he saw War-Axe riding, ritual scars white on his breast. He heard hooves and a wild yelling, and he saw Whip-Owner going past him to the picket-line with a knife in his left hand.

The Indians ignored the startled soldiers but drove instead at the cavalry horses which reared up against the picket-rope until it parted under the slash of Whip-Owner's knife. Nathan Donethegetaway swung his carbine by the stock, stumbled and struck nothing but the air. The frightened animals swayed, with their heads up and their teeth bared. One broke free to the prairie and ran before War-Axe's waving blanket. Another shied across Whip-Owner, and he shot it in the throat. But the rest were held together by the upraised arms of Salem and Nathan Donethegetaway.

Salvation Calhoun, swearing, ran after the Indians, emptying the chambers of his pistol at them, but they disappeared unharmed into the breaks, and soon even the dust of their passing was gone.

The shot horse lay on its belly, neck and head on the ground, coughing blood. Byrne walked across to it and killed it, and then he turned to the troopers. They stood together, their eyes white, suspenders hanging over their hips, and he wondered why the Comanches were such fools not to come back and strike again. It was Salem who brought the troopers from their shock, calling to them calmly, ordering two away to bring down Riddle's body, another two to look-out, and the rest to picketing the horses.

Riddle was laid by the water and a folded blanket was placed beneath his head. He had been shot through the body, the bullet passing across the depth of his chest. He was dying rapidly and the expression on his face showed that he knew this and faintly resented it. Donethegetaway bathed Riddle's cheeks and forehead, and cried. The trumpeter made two attempts to speak, looking up to Byrne and to Salem. At the third attempt he died.

He was buried in a shallow grave scooped out of the earth by spoons and knives, and as many white stones as could be gathered from the banks of the stream were placed upon it afterwards. Fragments of the committal service, dimly remembered, were paraphrased by Byrne into two sentences which he hoped would be fitting.

'Lord God, in this lonely place we commit to Thy care the body and soul of Trumpeter Absalom Riddle, Company M, Tenth Regiment of Cavalry, with which he was serving his second enlistment in the Army of the United States. He was a good soldier and deserves Thy mercy.'

He looked up from the grave to the ring of troopers, and it occurred to him that, with the exception of Salem and Attucks, this was perhaps the first time they had seen a comrade killed and had seen him buried. He tried to remember his own feelings on such an occasion, for he wished to say something that would soften the grief he saw in their faces, but he could remember nothing, not the feelings, not even the occasion. Although this disturbed him momentarily he knew that in time it would be the same with them, that they would come to accept another man's death as a rehearsal of their own.

The trumpeter's personal property was little. Salem brought Byrne the man's twist of tobacco, dice, a pack of Mexican playing-cards, and a few coins. There was also a slip of paper, finger-greased and worn through at the folds. Byrne put on his spectacles and read the browned ink with difficulty.

> H.Q., Dept of the South,
> Port Royal, South Carolina,
> 30 August 1862.

The bearer, Absalom Riddle, a private in the First Regiment of South Carolina Volunteers (Coloured), lately claimed as a slave, having been so held in hostility to the United States, is hereby, agreeably to the Law of the 6th of August, 1861, declared free for ever.

> D. Hunter,
> Major-General, Commanding.

Byrne passed it to Salem, who held it in his hand silently after he had read it. 'Declared free for ever,' he said at last. 'It's a good epitaph.'

'Do you know his folks, Salem?'

The sergeant smiled thinly. 'This is a *coloured* regiment, Lieutenant. Slaves didn't have folks.'

'The question had to be asked,' said Byrne.

'Oh, yes. Will the Lieutenant allow me to carry the bugle?'

'Of course. Salem . . . I'm sorry about Riddle. He was a good man.'

'Most of us get to be good when we die, Lieutenant. Even niggers.'

'Get them mounted, Sergeant,' said Byrne wearily.

Nine horses and ten men. An officer and a scout, a sergeant, corporal and six privates. Byrne told Salem to arrange for the troopers to take turns in being spare man, riding double in relays. He carried Conception's carbine himself, and gave Riddle's to Salem. The trumpeter's canteen he looped over the pommel of his own saddle. He sent Attucks and Honesty out to point, with instructions to proceed cautiously, to fire two shots from the pistol as soon as they sighted the Comanches, if they sighted the Comanches, and to retire immediately.

He looked back at the remaining men, mounted by files – Salem and James, Calhoun and Donethegetaway, Cato Brown and Cometoliberty riding double. He frowned at the thought of these two inexperienced boys on one horse, but decided that it were better soon than later. The faces of all of them were burnt, the skin peeling from raw patches of flesh. Their lips were thick and blue. He looked ahead to the rolling country and the red-brown escarpment, the yellow grass moving, and the loneliness of it all emptied his spirits. He raised his right arm in the habitual gesture, brought it forward without calling, and moved off at the walk.

The air was hot and windless. Low in the pale green sky, and far to the north was a tufting of white clouds. They promised no rain. At mid-morning, and almost against his judgement for he should have waited until noon, he ordered half a canteen of water to be poured in each trooper's hat and given to the horses. He then took the brandy jar from the medicine pack, soaked a corner of each man's bandanna, and told him to suck it as he rode. He was hoping that Nasthoe, who had gone ahead two hours before, would find water. He hoped for this with more faith than certainty.

The Comanches had made no attempt to hide their trail. They had ridden across every patch of grassless earth to leave prints, and sometimes, as if they believed this might not be obvious enough, they had tied grass-clumps into knots, arranged horse-droppings into circles or arrows. These signs had no meaning for Byrne, and he doubted whether the Indians intended any, they wished only to entice the patrol deeper into the badlands.

When Nasthoe returned it was with his head turned back over his shoulder. He grumbled to Byrne. He could follow the trail with the soldiers, he said, and he had no wish to be cut down by the Comanches when he was alone. A man liked to die in company, he said. He was confident that they were all going to die soon, the Comanches included, and when the patrol nooned the Wichita sat alone in the shadow of his pony, keening to himself softly.

Byrne took his shoulder, 'Water, Nasthoe. Did you find any water?' But the old man shook his head irritably.

Once that afternoon the Comanches showed themselves, a mile away, appearing one by one along a rim, their ponies nose to tail, their outlines sharpened by the slant of lance and gun. The point men came back in answer to the twirl of Byrne's hat. He focused his glass on the Indians. There were six of them and there was no sign of Davy. They made no movement, and Byrne had the odd feeling that they wished the patrol to come there to the spot where they waited. At last, and one by one, the Indians turned their horses and dropped down on the far side of the rim.

Byrne gathered his horse, punched the air twice, and put the patrol to the trot. The air was suddenly full of excited noise, the thud of hooves, the creak of leather, the singing of bridle chains and the ring of canteens. But the horses could not hold the pace for more than five hundred yards, and he slowed them to a walk again. '*Glory be!*' cried Attucks.

Below the gentle rim Byrne sent Salem and Nasthoe to the top, while he kept the patrol ready in skirmish line with holsters unbuttoned. The Wichita and the sergeant went up slowly, a hundred yards apart, and when they reached the top they rode as slowly towards each other. They looked away to the south-east and then Nasthoe jerked his hand to the north, dismounting and pulling his horse. Both men seemed to be lifting stones from the earth, and Salem stood up and waved his hat across his head.

They had found a grave.

Still horsed, the patrol gathered about it, their shadows falling across it in blue-purple bars. The grave was shallow, not more than two or three feet deep, and it had been loosely filled. The stones which Salem and Nasthoe had moved lay on either side, and in the centre of the hole was a small bundle wrapped tightly in Quasia's scarlet blanket. Byrne dismounted. He looked up at the troopers, scarcely seeing them. 'A knife,' he said thickly, his arm extended and the fingers trembling until they felt the haft of a knife placed in them. He bent over the bundle and cut the rawhide.

The blanket fell away. Davy's body had been bent at the hips, the knees drawn up to the chest so that the chin rested upon them. In this position had he been bound tightly. His face was covered with vermilion paint, the pale hair brushed forward over the eyes which had been closed with clay. Between the boy's feet was his one possession, the whistle that Attucks had made him. There was no wound, no mark on his body. He had just died.

Nasthoe was impressed. He nodded his head. 'Good!' he said. 'Good boy. Comanche think he good boy. Bury well, like Comanche bury.'

'*And may Christ forgive them!*' cried Byrne.

'May Christ forgive us all,' said Salem softly.

'And Amen!' said Attucks.

The rest of the patrol dismounted, and they stared at the body hopelessly until Salem took the knife from Byrne's hands and cut the thongs that bound the boy's body. He could not straighten the limbs, and Byrne, suddenly angered by the obscene wrestling, swore at the sergeant. 'Let him alone. Cover him up, damn you!'

Salem and Nathan Donethegetaway gently wrapped the blanket about the child, piling up the stones and earth again. Byrne knew that the troopers were staring at him, waiting for him to speak over the grave as he had spoken over Absalom Riddle, but he could say nothing, and when he finally looked at them he saw that their puffed and cracked lips were moving soundlessly.

'Mount up,' he said.

Attucks held out his hand, palm uppermost. On the pink skin was the whistle. Byrne took it and put it in his pocket. 'Mount up,' he said again.

They stared at him as if they were afraid of him, even Salem, and he pointed a finger at the grave. 'We'll kill them,' he said calmly. 'We'll kill them all. Mount up, I said!'

Nasthoe shook his head, and he too pointed at the grave. 'Good sign,' he said. 'Boy dead. No hunt Comanches any more. Now go back to fort.'

Byrne could see, by the faces of the troopers, that they were thinking this too. He took his pistol from its holster. 'Nasthoe, you talk like that again and I'll shoot you.'

'Shoot,' said the Wichita. 'You mad. Damn-fool mad.' He sat down on his heels with his face to the east and he sang. He looked up to the sky, and then he placed his hands on the earth. Byrne was surprised to see that the old man was crying.

'Sir . . .?' said Salem cautiously.

Byrne looked at him and then at the rest of the patrol. 'We're going on,' he said. 'We're going on because I say so. We're going on because that's how I see my duty and yours. It's not customary for an officer of the United States Cavalry to debate his duty with enlisted men. I don't propose to do so now. If any man questions my orders in future I shall believe myself justified in shooting him. Now, *mount up!*'

For a moment more they stared at him, and saw his hot eyes returning their stare from a blistered, bearded face. He returned his pistol to its holster, tightened his bandanna about his throat and pulled down the brim of his hat. Nathan Donethe-getaway was the first to mount his horse, and then the others followed slowly.

The earth had the astonishing beauty of most cruel things in nature. Its primary colours were abrupt and uncompromising, but the heat-twisted air above it was pastel-shaded. The earth was hostile with rock and twisted bunch-grass, yellow-dry brush and whitened stones. It was hostile and it promised further violence from every pleat in its horny hide. Byrne should have known what would happen, perhaps did know, even though he had withdrawn the point men. The patrol had ridden two miles from Davy's grave when the Comanches came out of the ground, pony after pony bounding upward with its rider yelling. But they came out too soon for overwhelming surprise, and Byrne had time to shout '*Dismount!*', waving his arm from left to right for a skirmish line.

He knelt on one knee, and he heard the thud of men falling, the snapping as carbines were cocked. He heard the soothing voices of the horse-handlers, and when he shouted '*Aim!*' he heard the butt-plates striking the buckles of the troopers' suspenders. Then the wave of Comanches halted, turned and rode away jeering, disappearing into the land again.

'Mount!' said Byrne. 'Walk march . . .'

Three times this happened before dusk, and each time the Comanche line swerved away before engaging. It became obvious that they had no intention of fighting, but wished to exhaust the troopers if possible. In this they were partly successful, but Byrne saw, with sour satisfaction, that their own ponies were tired, their flanks caked with yellow sweat-foam, and their last charge was made at no more than a canter.

When the sun went down like a rolling firework the patrol dry-camped, and heard the Comanches speaking to each other throughout the night, using the voices of owls and coyotes.

Byrne sent Nasthoe out, but the Wichita quickly returned, saying that he had seen nothing. He was frightened, and Byrne believed that he had done no more than crouch in a draw just beyond the rim of the camp fire.

Byrne entered the date in his notebook, an assessment of the patrol's strength and its approximate position so far as he could judge.

Ten men and nine horses, none of us capable of much more. The Indians push their horses harder than we do, but they carry less weight and are bred for this country. The Indians know the effective range of a Springfield carbine. They have two or three repeating rifles but did not use them today. Their damned pride. Must touch an enemy.

It doesn't matter whether you were right or wrong after you found Davy's grave. The decision was made and you have to justify it. You have got to be right. You have got to kill them all, otherwise what will have been the point of it all? That isn't it either. You *want* to kill them. How do you tell her about Davy?

Riddle dead. A strange man. What age was he? Never really knew him. How well do you know the others for that matter? He smiled once. You'll remember him as the man who smiled once.

Every time you write in this damned book Salem watches you. It seems to amuse him.

In the morning the men had three cups of water between them, and two full canteens were given to the horses. They ate a little jerked beef, and another half a cup of water was used to make biscuits with some of the *comanchero's* flour. Honesty, Calhoun and Brown complained petulantly of sore mouths, of teeth loose in the gums, and when they asked for salt to suck, believing it would tighten the flesh on their jaws, he swore at them for fools.

They mounted and rode into the sun, and Byrne tried to remember what he had been told, everything he had been told of the tactics of strategy of a Comanche war-party, its reliance on sudden surprise, on the unexpected attack and sudden withdrawal. He remembered that a corporal of the Seventh had once told him that Comanches, unlike the Sioux or the Cheyenne, would never stay to receive a charge, but would melt away before it, gathering again to regroup. A charge then, Byrne thought, would at least be one method of keeping the Comanches away. The words of the manual came into his mind. *'The charge is the decisive and most important characteristic of cavalry movement. The main conditions for its success are cohesion, rapidity, surprise and impetuosity and vigour in the shock.'*

He laughed, and at the ugly sound of it Salem pushed up beside him. 'The Lieutenant called?'

'No. Get into line.' Then, 'Salem . . .?'

'Yes, sir?'

'How are they?'

'God-damned thirsty, Lieutenant Byrne, sir,' said Salem. 'Is that all, sir?'

'That's all, Sergeant.'

Impetuosity and vigour in the shock . . . You've got to strike them some time. You've got to engage them. It isn't a question of keeping them away. When are you going to kill them?

The Comanches came out of the earth, yelling. Byrne did not call for a dismounted line. He waved his arm to the right and left and brought it forward, kicking at his horse and tugging out his pistol. He did not know whether the Indians were in range or not, he could scarcely see them through the sting of sweat in his eyes. He lowered the pistol, cocking it with his thumb, and he heard an answering clicking behind him. The volley was wild, and did no injury to the Comanches, but they broke from it, running. Byrne held up his arm and halted the patrol. *Are you mad, now? You do that again and you will kill the horses!*

He looked back, and was surprised to see that the troopers were grinning at him. Once more the didactic phrases of a manual slipped into his mind – *'Cavalry is an offensive arm, and, because of the improving effect on morale, offensive action by mounted men may sometimes be of more importance than the general tactical advantage of such an action.'*

He shouted to the patrol in furious delight. 'Damn you! Damn you, you Tenth Nubian Horse! I'm proud of you!' He faced his front abruptly, and with embarrassment.

In the heat of the afternoon sun the land swayed drunkenly. The refraction of light through the haze made distances deceptive, and directions distorted. There were times when the Indians looked like mannikins no more than two hundred yards ahead, and others when they appeared to be riding in the sky. The comic charge of the troopers had confused the Comanches, but it was not their confusion that pleased Byrne. He knew that they were tired, too, but if this thought gave him comfort he also knew that he should not under-estimate the cunning of Quasia. The Comanches might ride away and lose the cavalry whenever they chose. Quasia kept his men in sight and close to the patrol only because he wished to draw it deeper into this baked and cruel country.

That was the situation, and Byrne realized, none too happily, that all he could do was to follow, and follow, and still follow until the Comanches broke under the strain they were trying to impose on the patrol, or until they met it for a final clash. He did not ask himself whether Grierson would approve of what he was doing, and although now and then he wondered what the troopers riding behind him were thinking he ruthlessly suppressed such curiosity. He would have been surprised had he been told that this, however obliquely, indicated a faith in them he had not felt when the buffalo hunt had begun.

At three o'clock by his watch a horse at the rear of the patrol, a bay carrying James and Brown, went down on its knees wearily, pitching the men to the earth. He would not waste water on it, and he ordered Attucks to shoot it. The sound of the pistol rolled away over the wide land. He put his glass on the Indians, and saw that they had stopped too, waiting for the soldiers. He ordered a halt for thirty minutes, and he went from man to man, resting a hand on a shoulder here, slapping a back there, his tongue dragging out the old cheering jokes, the old obscenities that fortify a soldier's courage.

The appearance of the troopers was both comic and alarming. Their eyes were sunken and the lids purple. Incongruous black hair fluffed their cheeks. He moistened each man's bandanna with brandy and told him to inhale the fumes before putting it in his mouth. It seemed to revive them.

Towards the end of the half an hour he was sitting on his heels, with his hat brim pulled down over his eyes, when a scream brought him to his feet. The sun was in his eyes suddenly and blindingly, and at first he saw only a dusty blue melée by the horses, a flailing of arms. He ran towards it, and he saw Salvation Calhoun with his back to a horse and facing the other troopers. His yellow face was wet with sweat, his eyes swinging from side to side. His body was bent forward defensively and he held a knife in his hand. He spat out a passionate confusion of words *'Damn black nigger bastards . . .'*

The other soldiers sighed, a rustling moan of protest. Attucks stepped forward, his great hands reaching for Calhoun's throat. He cried, *'Ho!'*, and he lifted the mulatto by the neck, shaking him furiously.

'Attucks!' Before Byrne could get to the corporal, Salem hit Attucks on the side of the skull with the barrel of his pistol. The blow was delivered with terrible force, but it did not knock the man down. He staggered and released Calhoun, who dropped to the ground, clawing desperately at his throat. The corporal turned to Salem, his eyes red-rimmed, and his tongue running along his lips. There were tears on his cheeks.

'Jonathan . . .' said Salem, softly, and with great gentleness. 'Jonathan . . .' he said again, and he put his arm about the corporal's shoulders, turning him so that their backs were to the others.

Byrne looked down at Calhoun. 'Get up!' he said, and when the trooper was on his feet, his hands kneading his neck, he added, 'You all right, bub?'

Calhoun nodded, his face distorted by pain and hate. Byrne did not wish to know how the fight had started, or why. He shouted 'Mount up!', and they pushed on into the sun.

Within an hour he realized that the Comanches were no longer ahead of the patrol, that they were nowhere to be seen, and he was afraid. He called for a dismounted skirmish line without knowing from which direction the attack might come. It came from the right even as the troopers went down on their knees with their carbines pointed to the left, and he yelled to them to change front. The Comanches' appearance was an eruption of vivid colour from a gully which Byrne had not known was there and which even his flankers might not have seen had he posted them.

Quasia led the charge, upright on his yellow horse, a copper-coloured centaur with an impassive Mongolian face and sunlight sparkling on the beads in his hair. The five other Indians were in line behind him, and Kills-Something, thinner now, was singing. The troopers had time for one wild volley before the Indians were on them, but a shot struck Whip-Owner in the chest, throwing his body backward. Quasia rode by Byrne, touching the officer lightly on the shoulder with his rifle and crying 'A-he, it is mine!' and then all the Indians swerved to the right, dropping down on the far side of their horses.

'Pistols!' cried Byrne, and in the volley that followed two of the Indian ponies stumbled and fell. One rider lay beneath his animal, the other got up and began to run, and ran for four or five yards before he was killed by a pistol-shot. And then silence, the dust falling and the Comanches gone. It had all happened in less than a minute.

A bloody, stupid minute, thought Byrne. He wiped the sweat from his face and looked at the troopers. Blood ran down Salvation Calhoun's left arm, following each extended finger and dripping to the earth, and the mulatto stared at it incredulously until Nathan Donethegetaway forced him to the ground and ripped his blouse from the wound. Crispin Cometoliberty walked towards Byrne, grinning childishly, one hand lifted as if there were something he wished to say. He placed each foot carefully before the other, and he was still grinning when he fell down, and lay on his back and died. His fat body was cruelly comic in death, but his face, no longer grinning, was calm.

They did not bury him, but covered him with what stones they could collect, and they listened silently to the croak of Byrne's voice reciting the committal. Crouched on one knee, two hundred yards to the right and left, the look-outs James and Honesty stared backward in grief.

Then Byrne went out to the two dead Indians. They were young, young enough to seem like girls, and because he did not recognize them he assumed that they must be Woman's-Heart and Broken-Neck. He looked at them with satisfaction, but curious to see that the expression on their faces was so much like that on Cometoliberty's. When he turned away he brushed against Nasthoe, who was waiting impatiently to scalp the Indians.

The patrol mounted, and rode on until another horse slid down on its belly, and died before it could be pistolled. The Wichita calmly drank some of its blood, and sat alone by himself while the carbines of the dead men, Riddle and Cometoliberty, and of Conception, were broken and discarded to save weight. Their empty canteens were looped to the saddles of Byrne, Salem and Attucks. Nine men and seven horses now, the patrol silently answered the forward swing of Byrne's arm and marched for another mile, scarcely conscious of the four Comanches hovering ahead of them. Then Byrne halted again. He ordered the horses to be linked, one to the other by lead lines so that their riders might rest in the saddle, and he told the walking men to get what assistance they could from locking their wrists in the cincha straps. He saw the humming, glistening clusters of buffalo gnats on the soft flesh below the horses' eyes, and he told all but the rider of the lead horse, Salem, to wrap bandannas about their horses' heads. While this was being done he stared at the waiting Indians. He heard Salem's voice but he did not understand the words, and he turned his face. 'What is it?'

'Let them go.'

Byrne brought both hands to his cheeks, forcing the fingers into the tired flesh. 'Into line, Salem.'

'Let them go, Lieutenant. There's no point in this any more. Don't you see that?'

Byrne rubbed his gritted eyes and looked at the mulatto with astonishment. Salem's pale face was darkened by a beard, his cheeks hollow and his eyes large. 'Damn you, Sergeant, don't tell me what to do! Get the men mounted.'

'Have it your way,' said Salem. 'Maybe it doesn't matter.'

Two hours before dusk they saw that a single Indian was waiting for them, standing by his horse in a little arena of sand

and grass. It was Whip-Owner. Where the carbine ball had hit him in the chest there was a great hole, and blood was congealed from it to his thigh. He faced the troopers with an axe in one hand and a rifle in the other, and when they were a hundred yards from him, and halted there, he turned to his horse, killing it with a blow of the axe. He pulled a blanket free from the carcass, fastened one end of it to the ground with a knife, and tied the other end to the string of his clout. He began to sing.

'*Pukutsi!*' said Nasthoe, running a dry tongue over his lips. 'Crazy man wishing to die.'

'What's he singing?' asked Byrne.

Nasthoe shook his head, and said something softly in his own tongue. He dismounted, and squatted beneath the neck of his horse, his eyes bright with admiration as he watched the young Comanche.

Whip-Owner had freshly shaved the left side of his head, and the cluster of three feathers hung over his right ear. His hair was unbraided, and he was naked except for the clout and calf-high moccasins. The horse he had killed, so that there could be no escape for him, was the red and white skew-bald that had once belonged to Brown-Young-Man. When he had finished his song he shouted to the soldiers, shaking his rifle and beckoning them towards him. This exertion broke open the wound in his chest, and although he dropped the axe and put his hand over the hole the blood ran through his fingers. He fired his rifle, holding it out in his right hand, and the bullet sang away over the troopers' heads. Byrne watched with nothing more than curiosity.

Nasthoe stood up suddenly and called out. The words sounded like a salute.

'Lieutenant, sir . . . ?' said Attucks.

'Let him be. He couldn't hit the side of a waggon.'

'No, sir, Lieutenant, but . . .'

'Let him be, I said.'

When Whip-Owner fell on one knee there was a cry of encouragement from his far-off friends. He heard it and staggered up, only to fall again, on both knees this time. He knelt there and fired again, but the muzzle of the gun dipped down and the bullet went into the earth.

Salem put a hand on Byrne's wrist, gripping it tightly. 'Kill him!' he said. 'For God's sake kill him, it's what he wants.'

Byrne shook his arm free. 'Let him die this way,' he said. 'That's what *I* want.'

Salem swore, and pulled his carbine from the bucket, but Byrne grasped it, forcing it down. 'Damn you,' he said, 'do you command this patrol?'

Whip-Owner fell backward on to his heels and lay on his side. This wind, broken by his body, whipped the dust in curls about his face, but his eyes were open, staring at the troopers. A great cry came from the distant Comanches, but although he must have heard it he could not rise. The rifle had fallen away out of reach, and the fingers of his right hand, grasping and clutching at it, seemed to be moving independently of his body.

Byrne dismounted, took out his pistol, and walked slowly towards the Indian. He stared down at the twisted face until the boy died.

For an hour Byrne kept the patrol in the saddle, formed up in line, waiting for the other Comanches to come down to recover Whip-Owner's body. He believed that they must do this, he almost willed them to do it. But they did not move until the hour had passed, and then they turned and rode on.

Then, too, Nasthoe took the scalp of Whip-Owner.

They had no water. Byrne could not remember when the last had been drunk. They camped that night where once was a wide lake of flood water. The floor of it was baked and broken into octagonal clay tiles at which the hooves of the horses beat desperately. Along the edges, among the sparse bunch-grass, there was sign of buffalo, antelope and wolves, the grey goose and crane, but the prints were old and had been there since the spring thaw. On the high ground to the east, where the grass gathered a little before being choked by rock, Byrne placed his look-outs, changing them every hour. A hole was dug with some difficulty, but although the knives and spoons and spurs managed to scoop up the clay to a depth of two feet no water was found, and the digging was abandoned. Night came quickly.

The troopers sat silently while the darkness thickened, the light of the fire on their faces. Their mouths were too dry, their lips and tongues too swollen for them to eat what little there was to eat. They sat staring at the fire, or lay on their backs with their eyes closed. Only Nasthoe was busy, skilfully and reverently dressing the scalp of Whip-Owner, stretching it across the jaw-bone of a wolf that he had found in the grass, oiling it with carbine grease and decorating it with tufts of the feather from his hat. He then tied it to the stock of his rifle.

Salvation Calhoun was in a fever. His shoulder was inflamed and puffed about the bullet-hole, and he called again and again for water. He called in a sad, strange way, throwing his voice sideways from his mouth like a child flipping stones across a pool. Byrne moistened the man's lips with a little brandy, with no conviction that this would do any good, but hoping that

Calhoun would be aware of the attention, at least, and draw some comfort from it. When he was not calling for water the trooper talked deliriously, a spate of words and names and incidents that meant nothing to Byrne, but which exposed the terrible bitterness of the mulatto's soul. He swore at white men and he swore at Negroes, and he blasphemously cursed his mother and his father. Byrne listened for some word of distant love or affection, of longing or pleasure, and when he heard none he was filled with pity and revulsion. When Calhoun lost consciousness Nathan Donethegetaway came and sat beside him, motioning Byrne away with a brush of his hand.

It was very dark. There was no break between earth and sky, and the night seemed to flow up about Byrne from beneath his feet. He did not sleep. Sleep, he was sure, would only increase the agony of thirst, for a man exhausted his saliva when he was unconscious. Thirst, and death by thirst, he reflected, had intrigued him in the past, as he had also been intrigued by the thought of death or wounding by gunshot. It had fascinated him in the way suffering always fascinates a man, becoming in the end a personal challenge, forcing him to ask himself how well or how badly he might endure it. He had not, however, expected this odd, light-headed indifference he was feeling, a clinical interest in what was happening to him. He was aware of the absence of moisture in his body, not just the dryness of his mouth and throat, the pain of every convulsive movement of his larynx. He felt the skin of his arms, his chest and belly. It was like hot linen. He knew that this was a beginning, not the end, that there was much energy and endurance left in him, and he wondered at the strength of it, and wondered if it were there in the troopers too.

He looked at his watch frequently, every quarter of an hour and every half an hour. Every hour he called the look-outs to relief, and took his own turn with them, welcoming the loneliness out there among the grass and the rock, recognizing in it a momentary relief, a holiday from his ultimate responsibility.

When he returned to the fire he debated this responsibility with himself, and where it took the form of a moral argument it no longer seemed to have a solution. The practical problem,

167

the desperate need to find water, was perhaps easier to understand. The Comanches, he was sure, knew where to find water in this hot country, but were deliberately avoiding it in the belief that they, and not the patrol, could longer endure thirst and exhaustion. In his turn, he was determined to make the opposite true. Once again, he did not see in this conviction proof of how great was the change in his opinion of the troopers.

Sometimes, when he no longer felt capable of rational thought, there were strange visions in his head, not visions of water, of ice or snow which he had believed would naturally come to torment a man in thirst, but visions of himself, as if he had arisen from the ground without taking his body with him. He clearly saw himself sitting there. He walked about the figure and saw his back, and this amused him, because the one thing a man never sees of himself is the small of his back. Yet Byrne saw his own quite plainly, and the white stain of the dry sweat between his shoulders, the pale blue stretch of his breeches over his buttocks.

Then he shivered, and with the trembling seemed to contract within his own body again. Now he saw the woman. He saw Anne Norvall as he had first seen her, on the ground in the centre of her skirts, her arm about her son, and her calm, honest eyes looking up to him. He saw her across the table in the lamp-light, her fair hair polished. He heard the gentleness and the strength of her voice as she questioned him. And he saw her on the horse crying *'Kill them! Kill them all!'*

And he saw things that had not happened between them. He saw them marrying at Fort Sill, standing in Grierson's quarters before Chaplain Grimes. He could not understand why it should be Grimes, for if anybody performed the ceremony it would have to be a priest, that much he thought he owed his mother's memory.

He looked at his watch. It was two o'clock. From the horse-lines there came a terrible sigh; he had rarely heard a sound so unnerving, and he had heard horses shrieking like women when hit by artillery fire. He groped his way through the darkness to the picket line. His own horse had died.

168

Half an hour later one of the troopers stood up from his blanket. Byrne heard the noise, and he heard the rattle of a man's voice saying 'Got to go, Lord ... Got to go ...!' He listened to it, to footsteps, wondering why one side of his mind was urging him to go and see what was happening. He stood up at last and shouted, but his voice was scarcely more than a whisper. He walked out into the darkness, stumbling over the caked earth and calling, but he heard no answer. He went up to the lookouts, but they had seen nothing and heard nothing, and he thought that perhaps he had dreamt it all.

But in the morning he saw that Miles James was gone. There was no sign of him on the bed of the lake or on the distant grass. Byrne's sense of loss was particularly acute. It was not that he had felt close to the boy, understood him or even liked him as he had liked Cometoliberty. Something intangible had departed with James, and it was some time before Byrne realized that the patrol had lost its voice, its songster and psalmist.

It had lost something more, it had lost its eyes, for Nasthoe too was gone. Salem reported this to Byrne while the lieutenant was still staring out across the plain in the faint hope of sighting James. The Wichita had taken his own horse and equipment, and also Salem's canteen.

'Why yours?' said Byrne bitterly. 'What the hell good would it be?'

'There was a little water in it. Not much. Half a pint maybe, that I was saving.'

'How did he know?'

Salem shrugged his shoulders.

Byrne knew that he should have expected this. There was no reason why he should expect the Wichita to display the same kind of suicidal loyalty he was now demanding from the troopers. Nasthoe was an old man, and old men cling tenaciously to life.

'Tell the others he's gone on a scout, Salem.'

'Maybe he has.'

'No. He would have told me. He's gone for good.'

'And what do we do?' said Salem. 'Lieutenant, sir!'

'We follow the Comanches out there. They know where

water is, I'd swear to Christ they do. We follow them until they *have* to go for it.'

'And then we kill them?' said Salem, after a long pause.

'That's right, Sergeant.'

Dawn had brought a faint breeze. The soldiers turned to face it, their mouths open, but it was a dry wind, dry with dust, and it brought them no comfort. They did not speak of Miles James. They looked at his deserted saddle and blanket, and they looked across the wide horizon with melancholy eyes. Byrne thought he knew the point their emotions had reached, a point where a man, even with the best heart in the world, finds it impossible to expend more than so much sympathy, so much concern, being himself too desperately involved in the effort to survive.

When Byrne walked through the bivouac, hoarsely exhorting each man to action, he saw Honesty behind one of the horses, weakly making water into his cup. Byrne halted with shock, he had not believed things could have got this far. The boy had drunk before the lieutenant got to him and knocked him down. Honesty fell on his face, the cheek rasping against the earth, and he looked up at the officer with an expression in which pain, anger and apology were mixed. '*You fool! Damn you, you fool!*' shouted Byrne. 'Can't you wait? Don't you trust me?'

The answer to both questions was plain on Honesty's face.

Seven men and five horses now. Salvation Calhoun, his body too dry to sweat any more, but with fever hot in his angry eyes, was strapped to one saddle. Byrne ordered Brown, Honesty and Donethegetaway and Attucks to mount the others, and he swore for the first time at Nathan when the old man seemed inclined to refuse. Far off, how far it was sometimes difficult to judge, waited Quasia, Kills-Something and War-Axe. Byrne stared at them malevolently, wondering whether it would be possible to kill them from here, but the admonitory words of the musketry manual slipped smugly into his thoughts. *As a general rule independent fire is ineffective against the target of a standing man at 600 yards, or a horseman at 700 yards. Volleys by squads should not be ordered against a line equal to four men or more at distances of 600 yards or more.*

The Comanches must have read the manual, they were at least half a mile away.

'Walk march ... *Ho!*' The walking-men and the club-headed horses staggered towards the Indians, who themselves turned and moved into the sun. Byrne walked erect at the head of the patrol, his blouse pulled open to the waist, his face burnt and blackened, his beard grey. Salem walked beside him with lips that were puffed and cut, and Byrne guessed that the sergeant had been biting them to suck blood. He tried this himself, but the pain, when he touched his lips with his teeth, was too great.

The riders ahead had ceased to be Indians, or even men. He was involved with them in a macabre and deeply personal act of destruction, and although it would have been logical for this moment of mutual annihilation to have been reached at once, a persistent and crazily sane desire for survival kept them apart in pursuit. They moved across the hot earth slowly, so slowly that they seemed stationary.

An hour before noon by his watch Byrne halted and wet the troopers' bandannas with the last of the brandy, and then he threw the bottle away. Salvation Calhoun was dead, his body sagging against the straps that held him in the saddle. He was cut down, and the rotting stink of his wound made Byrne flinch. He was laid on the ground with his arms across his chest and two pebbles on his eyes. He took with him into death all the secret reasons for the bitterness that had sustained him while he was alive. Salem mounted his horse and they rode on, six men and five horses, and the Comanches still half a mile away.

At two o'clock they halted again because George Honesty was obviously mad. He had begun to sing, a cracked, unmelodious noise, and then he tried to fire his carbine at Attucks. The gun was taken from him gently, and he was helped from the saddle. He went mad like a dog that Byrne had once seen, an animal that turned and turned in hopeless pursuit of its own tail. So Honesty turned, clutching, his eyes wide, and his mouth open, until he fell down and died in Salem's arms.

Byrne was sure now that he was himself mad. He saw faces

clearly in the heat ahead. He saw Grierson fluffing out his brown beard to tuck the violin beneath it. He saw his father's face flushed with hate of the English, his mouth open in sound-less anger. He saw the faces of men who had once been close to him in friendship, but whom he could remember now by the names of battles only. He saw Anne Norvall calling upon him to kill the Comanches.

He was able to escape from the torment of these only by turning back to the men behind them. He looked at them, at Brown, Donethegetaway, Salem and Attucks, and he felt a tre-mendous and dispiriting affection. He floundered from one to another, calling their names, their Christian names. He walked for two hundred yards with his arms supporting the boy Cato Brown. He sang to them in a cracked and brittle voice, scarcely conscious of the words.

> 'O, the French are on the sea,
> Says the Shan Van Voght!
> The French are on the sea,
> Says the Shan Van Voght ...'

He waved his arms, crying to the soldiers to sing with him as he staggered.

> 'Will Ireland then be free?
> Says the Shan Van Voght.
> Yes, Ireland shall be free,
> Hurrah for liberty ...!'

'Hurrah for liberty!' he shouted, tugging at Attucks' sleeve. The corporal's black face was swollen and covered with flies. He did not seem to recognize Byrne, but he licked his bloody lips several times and echoed the cry hoarsely.

'You black heroes!' said Byrne, raising his hand in a salute. 'You damned, bastard, black heroes!' And he began to sing once more.

> 'Yes, Ireland shall be free
> From the centre to the sea,
> Says the Shan Van Voght!'

He heard his voice, but now it was not the thin, desperate sound it had been, but something strong and powerful. He listened to it, the rebel words roaring in his ears, no longer conscious of any movement in his throat or chest that might have produced them. He realized that he was not hearing his own voice at all, but his father's, and there was the old man sitting across the table, a fist beating the board in time with the music. The dragoons came over the dry-stone wall one by one, each with a sabre-flash of sunlight, and the air driven out of the horses' lungs in a cough as the hooves met the earth. His father shouted 'Kill them all!', and Anne Norvall, with her pale hair wild, shouted, 'Kill them all!'

Then he heard nothing and saw nothing but the rich blue sky above him and the rolling ball of the sun. He was lying on his back. He turned his head in slow agony and stared into the face of Salem, who was lying beside him. The sergeant's eyes glowed.

'Get them up. Get them mounted!' said Byrne. Salem did not reply, and the lieutenant pushed himself to his elbow. 'Get them up, damn you!'

Salem swallowed several times in an effort to speak, with pain, but with passionate determination. In little more than a whisper he said, 'I should shoot you!'

'Article Thirty,' said Byrne. 'Any soldier who thinks himself wronged may shoot his officer . . .'

He raised himself to his hands and knees, pausing there, and then forcing his back upright until he sat on his heels. He rubbed his hot eyes and he stared to the east. He bit the flesh of his forearm and sucked. The salt of the blood stung his lips but it strengthened his voice. 'Get up, Salem. They're still there. Get up.'

Somehow he got them all to their feet, kicking, tugging, ripping shirts, and when they were at last standing, leaning against the flanks of the horses, he flapped his arm drunkenly towards the waiting Comanches. 'Walk march . . . Ho!'

He walked for three yards, but heard no answering shuffle behind him, and he turned, rubbing his hand over his eyes. Cato Brown had slipped to the ground again and lay motionless on his face. Nathan Donethegetaway was weeping gently, his face lifted and the tears running past his ears. Attucks stood with his feet astride, his fists clenched and hanging before his groin, his fly-encrusted head swinging like an animal's. Salem had taken his pistol from its holster, holding it in his right hand and trying to cock it with the ball of his left thumb. It took him some time to do this, and Byrne watched with a cold and peculiarly professional interest. When it was done the sergeant raised the weapon in both hands, pointing it uncertainly at Byrne. The lieutenant looked at the round muzzle, the heavy foresight. *Why am I not afraid? Is it because I don't believe he'll fire, or because I don't care if he does?*

'You white trash!' said Salem.

'Attucks! Take the gun away from him.'

But the corporal looked at Salem and he looked at Byrne without comprehension. 'Hurrah for liberty!' he said very softly, and slipped to the ground.

'Nathan!'

The old man was still weeping, and still staring at the sky, his lips moving.

'All right,' said Byrne. 'Fire the damn thing. Go on!' He stepped forward and taunted the sergeant. 'What's the matter with you, can't you kill a white man, you nigger?'

'You said it,' whispered Salem. 'It's been on your tongue, and now you've said it.'

The pistol trembled in his hands, but the sound of a shot did not come from it. It came from the south, a single, booming explosion echoed by a drum-roll across the earth. Byrne mouthed the command 'Carbines! As skirmishers ...' without any sound breaking his lips, and then he realized that the shot had not come from the Comanches. He looked to the south. Against the swaying of the earth and sky he saw Nasthoe. Cato Brown pushed his grey face from the dust, and silently all of them watched the Wichita approach. There was a long and mournful cry from the Comanches.

When the scout rode up he was smirking with pleasure. A prairie-chicken hung from his saddle, and he held up three canteens. Byrne could tell from the swing of them that they were full.

A smudge fire was lit to drive away the insects, and Nathoe fed it with feathers from the chicken he plucked. The charred lips of the horses were moistened, their nostrils and eyes washed, and this was done several times and at careful intervals before they were allowed to drink. Coincidentally the men sucked bandannas soaked in the water. When Byrne finally held a canteen above each desperate mouth, almost counting the fall of the beads, Cato Brown cried out against the agony of swallowing.

The three Comanches watched from half a mile away, sitting in the shadows of their ponies, motionless.

Nasthoe told his story, making the most of his cunning, his guile and his skill. At dusk the evening before, while he dressed Whip-Owner's scalp, he had decided to leave. He told Byrne this without apology, but explaining that he in no way felt bound to destroy himself as the buffalo soldiers obviously intended to destroy themselves. He had guessed that there must be water to the south because the Comanches had deliberately avoided this direction. He had ridden a long way in the dark, and might not have survived had it not been for Salem's canteen. Towards the end he did think he was going to die, and then his horse had scented water. He dismounted, and let the animal find its way.

Twelve miles away, he said, jerking a black-nailed finger, there was water. Not much water, but sweet water.

'Eat,' he said, looking at the chicken, spitted over the fire on a cleaning-rod.

Byrne had no appetite. 'Do the Comanches know the water is there?'

Nasthoe shrugged. Of course.

Byrne, leaning against his horse weakly, looked at Salem. The sergeant's eyes were proud and hot. His lower lip was thick where he had bitten it, and but for the angry nobility of his eyes he would have looked like a pouting child. Byrne was quite unconscious of the fact that he was smiling gently at the mulatto.

'We go to water?' said Nasthoe, impatiently.

Byrne stared at the waiting Comanches.

No,' said the Wichita. 'Damn-fool follow now.'

'You giving me orders, Nasthoe?'

'We follow, we die, they die. Damn-fool thing.'

'Why haven't they gone after the water?'

'All *pukutsi* now, I guess. All crazy men wishing to die. We follow, we die, then maybe they go to water. Maybe die. Who cares?'

'And if we go to the water you found, will they follow?'

'Damn-fool likely.'

'Could they get there before us, Nasthoe?'

'I go see,' said the Wichita. He put on his hat, pulling its greasy brim over his ears. He looked at the chicken. 'Eat first, maybe?'

'No.'

'More water for pony.'

'No.'

'*Hou!*' said Nasthoe in disgust. 'All damn-fool now. Damn-fool Shot-in-the-foot come damn-fool back.' He took off his hat.

'All right,' said Byrne, and when the water was given there was scarcely half a canteen left.

'Give bringing-closer glass,' said Nasthoe, and it was handed to him.

The Wichita rode out towards the waiting Comanche, hunched in the saddle, his blanket about his shoulders, and the broken feather bobbing in his hat. He rode across the hard red earth until the colour of him passed and he was a black silhouette. He rode to within five hundred yards of the Comanches, dismounted, and sat on the ground with the glass to his eyes.

At first the Indians ignored him. Byrne could see only the ridged backs of their ponies, standing nose to tail, the dark clump where the Comanches sat. Then one man rose and walked very slowly towards the Wichita, calling out. He stood, and called out again, and when Nasthoe did not reply he turned, and went back.

The Wichita came back to the soldiers and he said, 'Eat now.' He was given a leg of the chicken, and then he asked for tobacco. Byrne had none, but there was a black twist in Attucks' boot, rock-hardened by the heat. Nasthoe first sucked this, and then tore a piece from it with his few teeth. The thought of a man having so much saliva to chew tobacco angered Byrne.

'All right,' he said. 'What about it?'

'Very bad. No water. One die soon maybe. We go. They follow.'

'What did that man say to you? Who was it?'

'Wepitapuni.'

'War-Axe was it? What did he say?'

'Say you die. Say why Nasthoe want die with you.' The Wichita picked his teeth. 'Good question,' he said, and grinned.

'What are they doing now?'

'Make medicine,' said Nasthoe. He said that Quasia had taken the sacred shield from its bag, which was something done only in battle, or in great emergency when its spiritual strength was needed. The white skin was painted with horses' tails and had a fringe of red feathers. There were three scalps hanging from it, said Nasthoe, white men's scalps.

'Big men,' he said soberly, and the thought saddened him.

'Would they stand and fight now?'

'No.'

'Then they'll follow us to the water?'

'Damn-fool follow,' agreed Nasthoe. 'You kill then?'

'I shall kill them then.'

The Wichita shook his head. 'Why?' he asked.

The canteen was emptied, and they marched to the south. Before the sun set another horse collapsed, breaking Cato Brown's arm. Nasthoe dismounted and cut the animal's throat, cupping the blood in his hands and drinking it. Attucks, Donethe-getaway, Salem and even the boy with the flapping arm, pushed about the dying horse to take the blood. Byrne would not join them, although he could not have explained why, for the running blood looked like water. He saw the animal's head stretched beyond the buttocks of the troopers. Before they closed, its eyes were like a cow's. Salem stood up, his face red-smeared, and he looked ironically at the officer.

While Cato Brown's arm was bound with wood and leather from the saddle, Nasthoe flayed the right haunch of the horse, cutting the blue meat into strips. Thus an hour, two hours passed, and all the time the Comanches waited, a thousand yards to the rear.

With darkness the five remaining horses were roped together, and the Negroes slept in the saddle as they rode. Byrne walked obstinately at Nasthoe's stirrup, refusing to take a relief, swearing hotly and incoherently when Salem offered to change places with him. In this fashion they travelled for perhaps five miles, from the hour the sun set until it rose again. At dawn Byrne took the bridle of the Wichita's horse and halted the patrol. He focused his glass on the land behind, rubbing first his eyes and then the lens, searching until he saw the Comanches. There were still three of them but only two horses now. He wondered if the other had died, or had been slaughtered so that the Indians might drink. Two of the Comanches were on foot. The third lay across the neck of one of the ponies.

Byrne closed the glass and looked at the patrol's horses. It was impossible to ride them any more, and he ordered the men to dismount, even Cato Brown, who retched as soon as his feet jarred on the ground. Byrne raised and lowered his arm and they moved to the south again. The night's march had worn his boots through to the soles of his feet, but he no longer felt any pain. Donethegetaway slung his boots about his neck and walked in bare feet like a plantation hand and seemed none the worse for it. Attucks had no shoes either, except those made from caked dust and blood. Salem put his arm about Brown's waist, urging him forward, whispering.

Byrne sang to them again, the croaking words of hate, his arm swinging across his body.

> 'O, the French are in the bay,
> They'll be here without delay
> And the Orange shall decay,
> Says the Shan Van Voght!'

Only Attucks' voice echoed the song. The rest were half-crazed by the salt taste of the blood they had drunk, their arms locked through the cincha straps, their bodies bouncing against the staggering animals. Suddenly Nasthoe's horse lifted its head and snickered, and the others raised theirs, too, nostrils flared and yellow teeth jutting. One broke into a hideous parody of a gallop, dragging at the lead-rope until it fell. Byrne shot it, and went from man to man, kicking and shouting. 'Get up! Get up, damn you! We're there!'

He heard hooves from the north, and saw the Comanches coming up at scarcely more than a canter, swinging to the right of the patrol in an effort to outflank it and reach the water first. They were still five hundred yards to the rear when the first pony, carrying two Indians, went down in a great flurry of hooves, the Comanches slipping away. The other man, it was Quasia, Byrne could see him plainly, and recognized the yellow animal, halted, and called out desperately.

Nasthoe shook his head. 'Damn-fool. Damn-fool warriors.'

The patrol moved on.

The water, when they reached it, came suddenly. One moment the earth stretched away unbroken. The next moment the water was there, a twist of it below red banks, black-deep it seemed and still, the earth about it pitted by hooves. Byrne could smell it, its strong, stagnant odour.

It took his strength and that of Attucks to hold the maddened horses, and he led them about the hole until they were downwind of it. He sent Salem away with three canteens, and when the sergeant returned the water was poured into the trooper's hats and given to the animals. Attucks wiped the wet felt over his face and yelled. Then at last they all moved in to the draw.

There was nothing, except perhaps the high banks and the shadows they cast, to explain why the sun had not long since sucked the water up into the bowl of the sky. It was not pure water, but they lay with their faces beneath it, lost in a cool delirium, until Byrne remembered the Comanches and leapt up. He ran back to the top of the bank, a carbine in his hand.

The Indians were six hundred yards away, three men sitting together in the shade of the droop-necked yellow pony. He stood up and focused the glass on them, but he could not see them clearly, the sun sparking and exploding on the sanded earth. He sat, and waited there, now and then bringing up the glass, until the sun set and the land turned red and passed into darkness. He heard a cry once, a long, throbbing call that might have been of anger, defiance or grief.

He smelt coffee. He turned, ready in anger to strike the man who had hoarded not only the beans but also a pot in which to boil them. It was Nathan Donethegetaway, standing just below the rise with the light of the fire behind him, his head to one side, and a cup out-thrust in his hand.

'You . . .' said Byrne, and he grinned and took the cup. 'Damn you, Uncle!'

He let them sleep that night, all of them, and he sat as sentinel on the ridge, looking out to the darkness in the north. He heard no sounds from the Indians. He heard only the wind most of the time, and Cato Brown's painful moaning. Once, too, he heard the anguished movement of Quasia's yellow pony, and he knew that the Comanches must have close-hobbled it to prevent it straying to the water. He wondered at the suffering of the animal, and then he remembered how he had smelt the water, and he knew that the Indians must smell it too, and must be suffering as much as the horse.

Salem came to him at dawn, bringing a canteen and some boiled pieces of a snake that Attucks had found and killed. The sergeant was naked to the waist, and he had wrapped his feet in torn strips of his blouse. He sat on his heels silently, now looking at Byrne, and now staring out towards the Indians.

The dawn light tipped over the eastern rim and flooded in mellow gold across the land. Two of the Comanches sat by the horse. The third lay on the ground and appeared to be wrapped in a blanket. Byrne raised his glass, cursed and rubbed the lens with the ball of his thumb. He saw Quasia and War-Axe quite plainly. The dead man, then, was Kills-Something, the fat murderer of Jinny.

'What are you going to do?' Byrne noticed that Salem's voice had lost its familiar and faintly deferential mockery. He spoke as he might to one of equal rank, and one of whom he had no opinion, good or bad. When Byrne did not reply, he said, 'You could ride down there now and kill them. Isn't that what you want?'

'There's no need.'

'Are you afraid he'll kill you instead?'

Byrne faced Salem curiously. 'You could have shot me back there. Why didn't you?'

'I don't know. Perhaps I should now.'

'Maybe you've never killed a white man, Salem.'

'White man, black man. You think in two colours.'

'All right. But have you ever killed a white man?'

'It wasn't difficult.'

'Why didn't you kill me?'

'Not because you're white, if that's the consolation you give yourself. I wasn't sure. I'm still not sure.'

'Sure of what?'

'That what you've done is wrong.'

'My duty is to kill Quasia.'

'No,' said Salem earnestly. 'You forgot your duty long ago, man.'

'So I *am* wrong, after all?'

'No,' said Salem. He held his arms across his chest and rubbed the muscles of his shoulders. 'You may even be right. I'd like to know. I'd like you to tell me.'

'Why should I? Why the hell should I allow you to question my duty?'

'Duty again,' said Salem, and smiled.

'It's a good word.'

'It's an expensive one, the way you observe it.'

'Did you debate your duty before Fort Wagner?'

'No,' said Salem. 'Maybe because all it meant was getting up there and killing white men.'

'You enjoyed that,' said Byrne bitterly.

'I enjoyed none of it. I didn't hate them. I don't hate Indians, either. Nor did your patrol. Cometoliberty didn't hate Indians. *Those damn niggers,*' he said, mocking a white man's voice.

'I never felt that way about them, Salem.'

'You never felt enough about them one way or the other. You ought to have been proud of them.'

'I'm proud of them, now.'

'It's taken a lot of dead niggers to make you proud,' said Salem. 'It took a lot at Wagner too. Do we have to die like white folk to prove we have a right to live like them?'

'I'd like to know why you hate me,' said Byrne sincerely. 'Is it because I'm white?'

'No. Calhoun hated you because you were white. Did you know that?'

'I didn't.'

'He also hated Attucks because he was black. Most of all Calhoun hated himself for being neither black nor white. Put that way hate sounds damn silly, doesn't it?'

'Why do you hate me then?'

'I hate nobody,' said Salem angrily. 'I wanted to hate you, watching you tip-toeing across your conscience. But after watching what you've done on account of hating that Comanche I want no part of hate.' He suddenly pushed his carbine across to Byrne. 'Go down and shoot him now. Why don't you?'

'He can die of thirst,' said Byrne without emotion.

'You're not a man, any more. You're trash.'

'You're out of line, Sergeant.'

'We're all out of line, Lieutenant, sir,' said Salem with amusement. 'There's nothing in the manual to cover what you've been doing. But you'll probably get a medal for it, and damn you, in one way you'll deserve one!'

'You're a liar, Salem. You've hated. You've hated someone, or it wouldn't mean this much to you. Was it your master?'

'Slaves don't hate, Lieutenant, sir. They sing. They are happy. We were better off than white men in factories in the north, weren't we?'

'I've heard the argument. Was it true?'

'It was true and it was a lie, like most of the things people tell their consciences. My master believed it.'

'Did you hate him?' Salem did not reply, and Byrne repeated the question, knowing that the answer was a key.

'He was my father.'

'Did you hate him, Salem?'

'I suppose I did,' said Salem, looking away. 'For I killed him.'

Byrne said, 'I understand.'

'And you still want to kill that Comanche?'

'I shall kill him.'

'Then you don't understand.'

'I don't understand you, Salem.'

'Is that important?'

'It seems important to me at this moment. I don't like you much, Salem, but you're a good soldier, one of the best I've known, and it seems important to understand you.'

'How about the others? The dead ones. Crispin, and Riddle, the others. The blue-gummed nigger troopers. The ones you killed.'

'Them, too. But I didn't kill them, damn you!'

'You want to understand what I'm trying to say?' asked Salem. 'Then ride out now. All of us. Leave the Comanches to their water and let them go. It'll be a beginning for you.'

'I've got to kill them.'

Salem shrugged his shoulders. 'It doesn't matter. Who cares what happens to us, to you or that Comanche?'

Byrne laughed.

'The Lieutenant is amused,' said Salem sullenly.

'The *comanchero*, Guaneros, said much the same thing.'

Salem sat up, his manner and his voice changing. 'Something moving down there, sir.'

Byrne put his glass on the Indians. One was astride the yellow horse and taking a rifle held up by the other. Byrne shouted over his shoulder. 'Carbines ... At the double!' And he heard the scuffling of feet, the heavy breathing, as Attucks, Donethegetaway, and Nasthoe came up to the rim. He looked back and saw Cato Brown, lying with his back against the wall of the bank and his eyes closed.

Nasthoe rubbed the edge of his hand beneath his nose and muttered. 'Give bringing-closer glass,' he said, and when he had looked through it he nodded. *'Pukutsi!'*

'Quasia?'

'No. Wepitapuni.'

War-Axe walked the horse up and down, raising and lowering the rifle as he sang. Then he turned the animal towards the soldiers and kicked it into a weary canter.

'Crazy man,' said Nasthoe, picking his teeth. 'Gun. No bullets. Wishing to die.'

The Indian's pony fell a hundred yards from the soldiers, and lay there with its neck stretched. War-Axe got up slowly. He left the rifle where it had fallen, and he took a knife from his waist instead. He was close enough for them to see his hollow cheeks, the valleys of his ribs, the red hole of his mouth, and his lips making soundless words. At last he opened his arms, lifting his face. This time they heard his voice. Nasthoe stood up and shouted a reply.

'He blind,' said the Wichita when he sat down again. 'Too much sun maybe. Ask where buffalo soldiers are. Damn-fool me tell him.'

The Comanche stood for a moment with his face turned towards the rise, and then he began to run with the knife upraised. Salem shot him calmly.

'Shall I kill the other one now, Lieutenant, sir?' the sergeant asked politely, the carbine held across his chest.

Byrne looked at the body of War-Axe and did not reply. Nasthoe grunted with approval. He walked down with his knife unsheathed, and he had one foot on the Comanche's back, his fist twisted in the scalp-lock, when Byrne shouted, 'Leave him alone! Damn you, *leave him alone*!'

'He's dead,' said Salem gently.

'I know that. But get that heathen back here!'

All afternoon Byrne remained alone on the rise watching Quasia. The heat was intense, and sometimes the dust and the rocks and the grass before him were twisted into fantastic images. Once Salem brought him a canteen of water, and seemed inclined to talk, but after asking about Cato Brown and hearing that the boy was as well as could be hoped, Byrne ordered the sergeant to return. He nursed his loneliness jealously, his eyes held by the distant figure in the dust.

The lower rim of the sun was close to the earth when Quasia stood up. Byrne rubbed at the lens of his glass and put it to his eye. The Comanche was stripping himself to the clout and painting his face with vermilion. When this was done he un-braided his hair, combed it carefully, and braided it again, leaving the scalplock hanging over his chest. He took the sacred shield from its bag and, unarmed, began to walk towards Byrne. As he walked he sang, and sometimes the words were lost in his throat and sometimes they came powerfully from his mouth. He walked steadily, and the shield in his left hand went up and down with the rhythm of his voice.

When he was a hundred yards away Byrne stood up, cocking the hammer of the carbine. He heard a scuffle of feet beside him.

'Sir . . .?'

'He's coming, Sergeant.'

In the scarlet mask of his round face Quasia's eyes were black. He held the shield above his head, its white hide and the blue horse-tails painted upon it. He sang loudly now, and he did not halt, although he must certainly have seen the carbine raised to Byrne's shoulder. He walked on until he was twenty yards from the soldiers, and there he stopped. He looked away over their heads, and he sang still, his hand on his breast. Byrne aimed at the splayed fingers, but his eyes were lifted from them to Quasia's face.

'Kill him then!' said Salem. 'What does it matter?'

The butt of the carbine dropped from Byrne's shoulder, the stock slipped slowly through his fingers.

'I can't.' He said this as if he could not believe it himself.

'Then maybe you want me to do it for you?'

'What did you say?'

'Maybe you'd like me to kill him for you?' repeated Salem harshly.

Byrne shook his head. 'No,' he said.

He threw away the gun and looked at his empty hands. He picked up the canteen and walked down to Quasia.

MORE ABOUT PENGUINS
AND PELICANS

Penguinews, which appears every month, contains details of all the new books issued by Penguins as they are published. From time to time it is supplemented by *Penguins in Print*, which is a complete list of all titles available. (There are some five thousand of these.)

A specimen copy of *Penguinews* will be sent to you free on request. For a year's issues (including the complete lists) please send 50p if you live in the British Isles, or 75p if you live elsewhere. Just write to Dept EP, Penguin Books Ltd, Harmondsworth, Middlesex, enclosing a cheque or postal order, and your name will be added to the mailing list.

In the U.S.A.: For a complete list of books available from Penguin in the United States write to Dept CS, Penguin Books Inc., 7110 Ambassador Road, Baltimore, Maryland 21207.

In Canada: For a complete list of books available from Penguin in Canada write to Penguin Books Canada Ltd, 41 Steelcase Road West, Markham, Ontario.

GLENCOE
John Prebble

'You are hereby ordered to fall upon the rebels, the Mac-
Donalds of Glencoe, and to put all to the sword under
seventy.'

This was the treacherous and cold-blooded order ruthlessly
carried out on 13 February 1692, when the Campbells
slaughtered their hosts the MacDonalds at the Massacre of
Glencoe. It was a bloody incident which had deep repercus-
sions and was the beginning of the destruction of the Highlanders, the end of which John Prebble has described in
Culloden and *The Highland Clearances*.

'Mr Prebble's description of men and events and scenery is
evocative and powerful. His research has been extensive and
thorough' – Corelli Barnett in the *Sunday Telegraph*

'Tells the old story excellently. There is colour but not too
much of it; imagination but under control; detail but not
overpowering' – *The Times*

CULLODEN
John Prebble

The explosion of a romantic bubble in a blind welter of courage and carnage.

For years the rose-ringed legend of Bonnie Prince Charlie and the black memory of Butcher Cumberland have blossomed side by side. Here from contemporary memoirs, letters, newspapers, and regimental order books John Prebble reconstructs the Common Man's version of the moorland battle and the months of repression and brutality that followed it.

Their bellies empty, their leaders at odds, the ground ill-chosen, the Highlanders were made sitting targets for the Royal Artillery at Culloden. This is the story of what ordinary men and women suffered in the Rebellion for a Cause that was never theirs.

THE HIGHLAND CLEARANCES
John Prebble

'Once the chiefs lost their powers many of them lost also any parental interest in their clansmen. During the next hundred years they continued the work of Cumberland's batallions.'

The closing sentences of John Prebble's *Culloden* provide an introduction to *The Highland Clearances*. This is the story of how the Highlanders were deserted and then betrayed by their own clan chiefs – and of how the famine and pestilence which followed their eviction from the glens to make way for sheep. While the chiefs became rich from meat and wool, their people died of cholera and starvation, or were forced to emigrate to unknown lands.

'... Mr Prebble tells a terrible story excellently. There is little need to search further to explain so much of the sadness and emptiness of the northern Highlands today' – *The Times*

THE LION IN THE NORTH
John Prebble

Eleven centuries ago Kenneth the Hardy emerged from a spate of savage battles as the ruler of a united Scotland. From that hour until Charles Edward Stuart saw Jacobite hopes forever crushed on the battlefield of Culloden, the 'long brawl of Scottish history' was fought to its bitter conclusion.

John Prebble, who writes with respect for England's oldest enemy, looks at the turbulent years of Scotland's independence, when treachery, hand in hand with noble ideals, stalked the glens, and no clan would compromise its pride.

The Lion in the North is narrative history at its colourful and dramatic best; Eric Linklater, writing in the *Guardian* about his native Scotland, warmly recommended it 'to all who enjoy a good story well told'.